✦ THE ✦
ORCHIDS
OF
ASHTHORNE
HALL

OTHER PROPER ROMANCES

As Rebecca Anderson
Isabelle and Alexander
The Art of Love and Lies

As Becca Wilhite
Check Me Out

PROPER ROMANCE

THE ORCHIDS OF ASHTHORNE HALL

REBECCA ANDERSON

SHADOW
MOUNTAIN
PUBLISHING

Library of Congress Cataloging-in-Publication Data
Names: Anderson, Rebecca, 1973– author.
Title: The orchids of Ashthorne Hall / Rebecca Anderson.
Other titles: Proper romance.
Description: Salt Lake City : Shadow Mountain, [2024] | Series: Proper romance | Summary: "Botanist Hyacinth Bell must brave the haunted Ashthorne Hall and uncover its secrets before she falls victim to its hidden dangers or before she loses her heart to the handsome and charming caretaker, Lucas Harding."— Provided by publisher.
Identifiers: LCCN 2023043177 (print) | LCCN 2023043178 (ebook) | ISBN 9781639932351 (trade paperback) | ISBN 9781649332523 (ebook)
Subjects: LCSH: Botanists—Fiction. | Secrecy—Fiction. | Cornwall (England : County), setting. | BISAC: FICTION / Romance / Historical / Victorian | FICTION / Romance / Clean & Wholesome | LCGFT: Romance fiction.
Classification: LCC PS3623.I545 O73 2024 (print) | LCC PS3623.I545 (ebook) | DDC 813/.6—dc23/eng/20231010
LC record available at https://lccn.loc.gov/2023043177
LC ebook record available at https://lccn.loc.gov/2023043178

Printed in the United States of America
Lake Book Manufacturing, LLC, Melrose Park, IL

10   9   8   7   6   5   4   3   2   1

❧

For Lisa and Heidi, who have guided and nurtured my work and my words for many years. Thank you.

LAMENT

My life, such as it was, ended at the sickbed in London.
Ravaged bones, weakened heart, ruined face. No hope left.
All I knew—gone, destroyed, lost to me.
Now I make my home in the deserted halls of Ashthorne.
The weeping of wind through stone masks my cries
As I await the time until I can, at last, disappear.

CHAPTER 1

Not until the screeching wind overpowered the sounds of the horses' stomping hooves did Hyacinth Bell pull back the window coverings in the jolting carriage. Though impatient for her arrival, she wondered what a wind so powerful could be doing to the landscape.

As it happened, almost nothing. The moors of central Cornwall were completely barren as far as she could see, and the wind could blow unimpeded across miles of fields without paying any attention to the earth, searching for something—anything—that stood higher than a sheep.

Hyacinth's carriage, for instance. The wind seemed determined to surround it on all sides at once. Nothing else marred the horizon as far as she could see. Not a building in sight. Hardly a tree.

The thought that she was riding in the highest point across the entire countryside made her laugh, a sound made slightly unhinged by nature's accompaniment of wailing wind.

Unsettled by the gale, she hummed to herself. As the noise outside the carriage pressed against her, humming was not enough. She sang. Even at the top of her voice, she was drowned by the volume of the storm. Was this what it felt like to go mad?

The wind roared, screeched, and rattled around her, giving her the feeling that even within the walls of the carriage, the very atmosphere sought to attack her peace. She knew the wind was not whipping her hair about her head like a ghost in a penny dreadful illustration, but she felt as though both her rationality and her hairstyle were holding on by a mere thread. Or a miracle.

Not that anyone but the driver would see her hair, or care if they did. Not until the stop in Suttonsbury village. Not until her meeting with Ashthorne Hall's temporary orchid caretaker, an elderly man who managed a village greenhouse. Hyacinth had agreed to go to his shop to pick up the last packages of soil preparations and instruments that Mr. Whitbeck had ordered.

He would also give Hyacinth any final instructions before she made her way through the gale to Ashthorne Hall and her new position. Her new life.

The horses' whinnies carried on the wind, another layer of shrieking adding to her unease. Hyacinth wondered how the driver fared in this monstrous wind, if he held his perch up on the driver's box by the strength of his will. For a moment, she considered pounding on the wall and calling out to him, but even if she could get his attention, he would not be able to hear her ask after his safety or comfort, so she pulled the window coverings tight and hummed again.

The almost inaudible sound of her own voice was less than reassuring.

She lifted the potted orchid from the seat beside her.

"Eleanor," Hyacinth said to the orchid in a voice of warm

3

confidence, "if you could see outside, you'd not recognize anything growing here. None of our hothouse friends could survive a night like this."

She did not raise the window cover to give Eleanor a peek at the moor; that would be silly.

The roaring autumn wind, she knew, could not last forever.

At least, she thought it could not. In fact, she was aware she knew very little about the weather patterns of Cornwall, to say nothing of its residents or their feelings about visiting botanists.

Once she arrived at Ashthorne Hall, she vowed, she would never again leave. A hundred years would be too soon for another carriage ride like this one. How grateful she was that most of the hundreds of miles she had traveled from Herefordshire had been by train. Only since Plymouth had she been inside this carriage, and only for the last half hour had she felt her excitement turn to anxiety. And that she could mostly blame on the infernal wind, which had alternated in pitch between a roar and a wail.

Hyacinth looked down at the note from Mr. Whitbeck in her right hand. Replacing Eleanor on the carriage seat beside her, she clutched the letter in both hands, the paper grown soft from dozens, perhaps hundreds of openings, followed by careful reading and refolding. After months of seeking employment and waiting, she was finally on her way to Ashthorne Hall.

She envisioned the stone edifice rising out of a grove of trees, chimney pieces streaming warm smoke and window glass reflecting surrounding sunlight. Having never seen the manor where she would soon live, she had created an image of her own devising by compiling the best parts of elegant houses she knew: rooflines and landscaping, trees and ponds and driveways, stones of warm golden hue.

How much of Ashthorne would match her imaginings? And what of the people living inside? She had little more than Mr. Whitbeck's note and seal to recommend her to the housekeeper and the caretaker. And it was possible they would be the only other inmates of the manor. The rest of the staff had either removed to India with the family or been let go to find other employment.

Her imagination gave her comfort, but she realized she might have to let go of her preconception. Her father had taught her that the ability to hold on to an idea was a very important skill for gaining knowledge and understanding, but he emphasized that an even more crucial skill was the ability to let a faulty thought go.

She had trained herself to treat her thoughts like precipitates, the solids that separate from a chemical solution: With a bit of agitation, things settle. Once they do, an observer has something to look at, to study, and to hold on to or reject as evidence suggests.

She hoped the housekeeper at Ashthorne did not hold too tightly to any false ideas about her.

Nothing in Hyacinth's bearing or stature identified her as either an expert botanist or a genius gardener. She looked rather like a tall schoolgirl, if one with a more than usual amount of dirt beneath her fingernails. But Hyacinth Bell was no child, and she had learned from the greatest scientific minds of the day. Her father, a viscount, had early in his peerage grown weary of days filled with receiving complaints and reporting them to the earl. In his leisure time, he gathered to his home men of science, and as he learned of ways to improve farmlands, increase crop productivity, and strengthen plants, he passed on all his understanding to his youngest daughter, who took to the lessons and the experiments with a passion and a consideration he had not expected.

He was delighted.

Hyacinth soon outstripped her father in her understanding, and with his blessing, she continued to study plants and propagation, flowers and seeds, and the maximization of crop yield. Before many years had passed, she had grown from a precocious child with a gardening hobby into a highly respected young lady, eager to share her knowledge and understanding with the farmers in her father's care.

After the death of her dear mother five years prior, Hyacinth took over care of the lady's orchids, and there found a gift and talent she had not anticipated. She soon became masterful in her work with tropical blooms. Many people thought orchids were difficult flowers, but Hyacinth soon realized that they had few needs: soil conditions, water, light, and air. Once you understood these, the care came rather easily.

Hyacinth's father recommended her to all who would listen as one of the greatest orchid experts in the country. She knew he spoke far too highly of her talent but appreciated the acclaim that surrounded her in English botany circles.

Mr. Charles Whitbeck, a magistrate and orchid enthusiast, had written to Hyacinth upon occasion, seeking advice for his impressive orchid collection. Mr. Whitbeck had plans to travel to India, and he invited her to come to his home at Ashthorne Hall and look after his hothouse in his absence.

"There is not much I shall miss while I am away, but I will rest easier if my treasured orchids are in your capable care."

Hyacinth had grown more excited by the day about the possibility, and her father believed the adventure would be a wonderful interlude before she settled down as the brilliant wife of some worthy man or other. And now, after months of preparation, Mr. Whitbeck was off in the tropics, and Hyacinth drew near Suttonsbury village, the town nearest to Ashthorne Hall.

Traveling through the ominous and unsettling storm, Hyacinth felt the minutes drag, as though the wind pressed her ever farther from the town. Just as she became certain she'd crawl out of her skin if she had to sit another minute in the jostling coach, she both heard and felt a knocking at the wall of the carriage.

"We're approaching Suttonsbury now, miss," the driver said. At least, that is what Hyacinth thought he said as the wind tore half the words from him and carried them away to crash against the cliffs and rocks of the wild coast.

A few more minutes brought them to the village's greenhouse, and at the horses' halt, Hyacinth threw open the carriage door, eager to escape the tight confines of the vehicle, even if it meant a drenching from the rain. She lifted Eleanor's pot from the seat and stepped down.

The wind had slowed enough that she could stand in front of the garden shop without her hair blowing completely loose from its knot. She looked up at the sign swinging from two metal chains attached to the roof: Gardner's Paradise.

At her knock, a man opened the shop's front door, and Hyacinth's first instinct was to back away. His shirt, covered with an open brown vest, was filthy. He looked at her sideways, squinting an eye, and a muscle jumped near his mouth, pulling his lip into a sneer.

"Closed," he said, as if she did not deserve a complete sentence. He began to shut the door. Was this the man Mr. Whitbeck wanted her to communicate with?

She wondered if she ought to simply get into the carriage and come back another day, but she had her instructions. "There is an order for Ashthorne Hall, I believe."

The man leaned out into the wind and rain as if inspecting her. "You the Whitbeck's new flower girl, then?" he asked with a growl. His breath carried more than a hint of whiskey. His glare, more than a hint of disdain.

His rude behavior made her wish she would never have to return here. But since it was the only garden shop for miles, she knew she'd need to come back. Perhaps she could salvage some of this bad first impression.

"Mr. Gardner?" she asked, holding out her hand and hoping she did not look as much a fool as she felt, standing in the rain.

Ignoring her proffered hand, the man shook his head and huffed in contempt. "I'm James. Gardner is out back in the greenhouse. He has your parcels. Walk on through."

Though relieved that this unpleasant man was not Mr. Gardner, Hyacinth felt James could do with a reminder of basic manners. He spoke to her as he would to a horse. But she chose to say nothing and simply followed him through the shop and out the back door. A glass garden structure glowed with the light of dozens of hanging lamps, warmer and more welcoming than any word from James had been.

The alleyway between the shop and the greenhouse was

a throughway for the night's wind, which gusted against Hyacinth's body and practically pushed her sideways. James rapped on the glass door and waited, his hand holding his hat to his head. He muttered something about locked doors that she did not try to hear.

Hyacinth watched through the glass as a figure scuttled toward them, becoming clearer as he approached. By degrees, she could discern his short, round figure, his hurried gait, and his full, white beard. Everything from his posture to his age to his stature spoke of the difference between him and his hired helper. James was large and slouching and sullen. The man hurrying toward her practically bounced as he jogged, and she saw his smile through the glass walls. By the time he opened the door, Hyacinth knew she would be fond of this man.

James muttered, "Whitbeck's new hire," and made a sound of displeasure. "Hope she finds the manor to her liking." He sounded anything but hopeful as he turned back to the shop.

Hyacinth was not sorry to be rid of him.

"Ah, Miss Bell. I'm George Gardner, and very pleased to meet you." With a warm smile on his weathered face, Mr. Gardner reached for Hyacinth's hands and pulled her into the safety of the greenhouse. He chuckled as he looked up into her face, as he was only as tall as her shoulders.

"Welcome, welcome. Come in out of all that weather, dear," he said. "I'm right glad you've found us."

A shock of white hair grew like a cluster of shaggy ink cap mushrooms from beneath his pointed red hat. His brown leather apron did little to hide his bulbous stomach, which seemed to shake as he laughed. With a hand still on her arm, he reached over and locked the hothouse door behind them.

"Can never be too careful," he said when he turned back. With a clap of his hands, he said, "Now. Can I talk you into a cup of tea and a comfortable seat before we get down to business?"

"I really must not keep the Ashthorne housekeeper waiting long," Hyacinth said. "But I hope we can share a cup and a visit on another day. I am sure you have much to teach me."

Mr. Gardner laughed again. Hyacinth believed it might be his natural response to most situations, and she decided she liked it a great deal indeed.

With a wink, Gardner said, "Oh, don't flatter me, young woman. I've nothing like the skill you're known for. Mr. Whitbeck sent word about you."

"Did he?" Hyacinth smiled at that. What might he have said? She was pleased her reputation impressed him enough that he'd spread it through the village before he left for India.

"Oh, aye. You're a right smart touch with the orchids, he tells me. And well you should be, for his collection is a masterwork. Far more than James and I could manage."

"Sir, I'm sure you kept the collection in good order since Mr. Whitbeck left," Hyacinth said.

Mr. Gardner nodded. "It's a beautiful lot he has, indeed. James would have liked to stay up at the manor, for he does fancy life at the big house. As I worked in the hothouses, he took to wandering. I believe he went looking for pirate caves." Mr. Gardner's laugh rolled out of him again.

"But you, Miss Bell, are perfectly suited for the work and the station. Between you and me," Mr. Gardner said, "when I took on the extra work at Ashthorne, I ought to have hired someone who knows more about plants. Or who is more polite to customers. Or who can manage to stay in the place he is supposed to be working." Mr. Gardner laughed again, as if his mistake in hiring his employee was a great joke.

If she knew him better, she might ask one of the many questions filling her mind. Why would Mr. Gardner hire someone so obviously unfit to help him in his work? But even though he led the conversation in that direction, she felt it would be rude to pry.

"Good help is often difficult to find," she said.

Mr. Gardner grinned and nodded, holding the sides of his ample stomach. "Mr. Whitbeck certainly got the best England had to offer when he found you."

Hyacinth began to make a polite denial, but Mr. Gardner gestured to the pot in Hyacinth's hand. "Have you already been to the manor, then?" he asked.

She shook her head. "Oh, no. This is Eleanor. She once belonged to my mother."

The emotion in her voice surprised her. Of course she loved her plant, but the feeling of loss and mourning caught Hyacinth off guard, and she put her free hand to her face as she attempted to steel herself against her grief.

Mr. Gardner seemed able to read her feelings in her face. He nodded gently and said, "And a fine-looking orchid she is. She'll fit right in with the others."

His affirmation was exactly enough to help Hyacinth move past her momentary sorrow.

"Thank you. Having her safe in the orchid house will be a relief to us both, I'm sure."

"We mustn't keep either of you waiting, then," he said, and they made their way to the rear of the greenhouse where he gestured to a stack of crates.

"I'll have my man James load these into your carriage. And perhaps your driver can assist us."

"I'm happy to help as well," Hyacinth said, lifting a small box from the top of the pile to prove her willingness.

Mr. Gardner immediately protested, but Hyacinth didn't give him a chance to stop her from helping. Pulling a crate from the pile, Mr. Gardner led Hyacinth back out of the greenhouse and to the rear of the shop. Mr. Gardner knocked and called out, "James, give us a hand with these parcels, if you please."

As the shop door opened, Hyacinth heard the younger man muttering even over the sound of the wind.

If this was the kind of person working in this village, she felt grateful at the thought of a deserted manor house. She would rather be alone than in the company of men like James.

Returning bearing several of the boxes, he continued to grumble. She pretended not to notice his unsavory language or the comment that may or may not have been about her. As she lifted her crate up to the driver, James came up behind her.

She moved aside half a step to avoid touching him.

He moved closer, standing far too close to Hyacinth's ear. "You'd do well to watch yourself in that old house," he said. "Don't go wandering. Place is haunted by spirits."

Hyacinth chose not to answer, but she stepped away from James and closer to Mr. Gardner. Ghosts? Did this man think her a child, likely to be frightened by silly tales?

She was glad he could not see the fine hairs on her arms rising in response to his warning, unsure if she was more frightened or thrilled by the possibility of a haunted manor.

She stayed between Mr. Gardner and the driver as they

moved the garden supplies to the carriage. With all four of them carrying parcels, it only took one more trip to the greenhouse before the packages were loaded. The driver retook his seat and held the reins as the horses stamped in the rain that had become a downpour.

Mr. Gardner handed Hyacinth in to the carriage. "Keep your eyes open up there at the manor. You must know places like that are full of ghosts," he said, still with a grin and a wink, but this time, Hyacinth's shiver was less enjoyable than the first. After that comment from James, Mr. Gardner's jest felt too real. She glanced over Mr. Gardner's shoulder, but James was nowhere in sight.

Mr. Gardner continued, "But that doesn't mean you've anything to fear. Everyone knows old houses are full of haunts. No need to assume the ghosts are of a wicked turn of mind. You might learn a thing from the Ashthorne spirits about making yourself at home."

He grinned, and his whole face folded in wrinkles and the lift of pink cheeks. "Of course, the coast has also been overrun with pirates for hundreds of years, and they are probably a different story. Do stay away from the pirates, Miss Bell. And please come see us when you next make a trip into the village. I owe you a cup of tea."

His silly pirate warning made her feel better; clearly, his stories were all in fun. She gave his hand a squeeze and thanked him for his help. "I would love to come back and visit."

Mr. Gardner nodded and closed the door. Seconds later, the horses were in motion, and once again, carriage full of garden supplies and head full of ghosts, Hyacinth was on the road to Ashthorne.

❧

LAMENT

So cold.
The wind blows unceasingly.
I miss the warmth of my strong, healthy body.
There is nothing here to give comfort but memories of
happier times.
The future holds nothing but pain.

CHAPTER 2

Rain lashed at the carriage. Hyacinth was grateful to be inside. Even with Mr. Gardner's mention of specters at Ashthorne, he was a delight, but the thought of his man James made Hyacinth's flesh crawl.

His threatening manner, the way he stood much too near, not to mention the stink of stale smoke and alcohol meant she would be quite happy never to see him again. Nor would she waste any more time thinking about him.

Closing her eyes, she imagined placing all thoughts of the unpleasant man in a shallow dish. Then she pictured her mind beginning to spin the dish, collecting the thoughts so she could dispose of them. She let her mind swirl, and, as she had practiced, she was able to dismiss the disagreeable thoughts.

She turned her attention to the window once again. Clouds thick enough to block any moonlight combined with the curves of the road made it difficult to discern the distance from town to the manor, but Hyacinth estimated somewhere between a mile and two. A reasonable walk if the weather was right.

The weather was anything but right tonight.

She cradled Eleanor's pot in her arms, whispering to the plant as they drove. She described what she saw from the carriage windows—although there was little to speak of—in an attempt to calm herself. "There, up on that rise. Do you see?"

She held Eleanor up to the window. "That poor tree, growing all alone. There is nothing nearby to protect it from this ghastly wind. Do you see how it bends? Do not worry. You will never be left alone to do battle with the elements. I will keep you safe."

She knew speaking to her mother's flower was a signal that she was lonesome, but she did not worry. Gentle Mr. Gardner, so like a gnome or a forest elf, would be a colleague for her, and additional human companionship was only a short carriage ride away. Surely she would make friends with the Ashthorne housekeeper, not that a new acquaintance would make her love her dear Eleanor any less.

As the carriage continued forward, Hyacinth squinted into the darkness.

A line of trees loomed out of the shadows. Nothing else on the moor grew as tall. These must not be natural growth, but she could tell they'd been planted generations ago. As the carriage approached, Hyacinth could see the manor's property was crowded with trees, full and tall, giving the estate a feeling of warmth and homeliness. Off to her right, she could make out a tiny light winking, and as she stared at it, the shape of the house seemed to draw itself on the darker canvas of the night.

Instead of intricate rooflines and innumerable chimneys, the façade of Ashthorne Hall rose like a blank wall, huge and rectangular, behind a fringe of scrubby trees placed either for decoration or protection. Those trees swayed in the constant wind, leaning first in one direction, then another. They did not seem to fare as well as the groves planted throughout the property.

Only one window showed any lamplight: on the top story of the house, a silhouette of a woman stood framed within the borders. The carriage swayed as it moved through the storm and onto the manor's curving approach. Hyacinth uncovered the opposite window, trying to keep her eyes on Ashthorne through the twists and turns, but by the time she could reliably see the house again, the upstairs window was dark, and the driver had pulled to a stop at the front entry.

"We appear to have arrived, Eleanor," Hyacinth murmured.

Rain and wind rocked the carriage, but there was nothing for it but to brave the elements and enter her new home.

Hyacinth disembarked, adjusting her skirts and gripping her hat to her hair as the driver unloaded bags and garden deliveries onto the drive. Glancing around for a butler or footman, Hyacinth realized there might be no one of that description on staff since the family was away. She reached inside the carriage for Eleanor and her valise, prepared to instruct the driver to take her bags to the door.

As she turned back to the house, she was startled by a stern-faced woman wearing a neatly pressed housekeeper's dress and holding a large ring of keys. Hyacinth jumped, surprised by the woman's silent arrival. Her valise dropped to the ground, but she kept tight hold of Eleanor.

"Miss Bell, is it?" she asked, and in the dark of the stormy night far from home, Hyacinth realized what a small name it seemed. Miss Bell. She could be anyone or no one with a name like Bell. For a moment, Hyacinth thought of telling her no. She could make up a different name, be whomever she wanted to be in this new place. But then she realized the question was merely a formality. It wasn't likely the woman was expecting a great many people to arrive tonight in the middle of this storm.

Hyacinth nodded and extended her hand.

The woman glanced down but did not take it. "I am Mrs. Carter, Ashthorne Hall's housekeeper. You may follow me."

Instead of mounting the impressive front stairway to the great dark door, the housekeeper moved to walk around the side of the house. Hyacinth tucked her orchid into her elbow and lifted a bag in each hand. The driver carried the trunk with two smaller cases stacked on top, and they followed the housekeeper along the path.

Turning the corner, Hyacinth began to understand the scope of the building. A great wide swath of gardens swept along the side and rear of Ashthorne Hall. Some flanked by hedges, some by groves of trees, the estate's parkland was vast. She'd grown up in a large and lovely country home, but this made her father's house feel insignificant by comparison. She stopped in her tracks, head lifted in the rain to take it all in.

Mrs. Carter tsked in impatience and motioned for Hyacinth to keep moving. "Stay close, if you please. You don't want to get stranded out here."

Hyacinth glanced at the driver, who followed her at a respectful distance, keeping his eyes on the ground. Would Mrs. Carter truly leave her behind? She hurried her steps, just in case, and in a few more moments, they stood in a warm kitchen, fire blazing against one wall and a spotless table before them.

"I wasn't sure precisely when you'd arrive," the housekeeper said, looking at Hyacinth from beneath a brow that, if not menacing, was certainly not gentle. Austere. Well, Hyacinth could manage austere. She lowered the cases she'd carried onto the floor.

"I regret any inconvenience. As I stated in my letter—" Hyacinth began, but Mrs. Carter interrupted her.

"I saw your letter, but trains are often late, and the moors can be unfriendly to coaches and wagons, especially during an autumn storm like this." She turned to the driver. "You may place the remaining parcels at the back door. If you'd care for a cup of tea, I suppose I can prepare one for you now."

If there was a less welcoming, less inviting way to offer refreshment, Hyacinth couldn't imagine it. Instead of correcting the housekeeper, she turned to the driver. "Thank you for bringing me here in a safe and timely manner, sir. Won't you sit down for a cup of tea before you bring in the packages from Mr. Gardner's shop?"

The man shook his head, shooting a glance into the dark doorway that led into the next room. "I'll be unloading at the door and returning now, thank you." A pause, then he looked at Hyacinth and added in a low voice, "Take care, miss. Keep your eyes open for what might be hiding." With a short nod to both women, he let himself back out into the night.

Hyacinth was sure her face reflected her surprise at both his warning and his hasty retreat. He had clearly heard the jokes from Mr. Gardner and threats from James in Suttonsbury village, and as much as Hyacinth eventually dismissed the ghost stories as quaint folklore, the driver obviously felt the full weight of her impending doom. When she looked to the housekeeper, Mrs. Carter shifted and glanced away, as if not wanting Hyacinth to know she'd been watching her.

Mrs. Carter did not renew her grudging offer of tea but lifted a case and stepped toward the dark hall. Taking a lighted candle from the table, she spoke to the darkness. "I'll show you to your room, then."

Hyacinth readjusted her grip on her bags and her orchid and followed the woman out of the kitchen. Immediately she felt the loss of the kitchen fire. A chill draft wafted in the dark hall, lifting the damp hair at the back of her neck and whistling mournfully. The candle was woefully inadequate for the task at hand, and as the women stepped into a widening corridor, Hyacinth felt engulfed by shadow.

The hallway stretched out for what seemed like forever, but eventually they reached a space where Hyacinth could not see walls on either side.

"Main entry hall," Mrs. Carter said, as if in introduction.

Hyacinth's eyes had adjusted to the dim glow of the flickering candle, and she looked toward the manor's front door, a dark smudge against a darker wall. Through tall windows she watched the dance of the windblown trees standing guard outside. Across the vestibule from the door, she could just perceive two grand staircases, rising out of the floor and curving upward to either side like wide leaves at the base of an orchid.

Mrs. Carter crossed the vast floor and turned up the elegant staircase to the right, and Hyacinth followed. Questions filled her mind as she climbed the stairs, but she asked none

of them. The housekeeper's reticence did not welcome conversation. At the first landing, Mrs. Carter led Hyacinth to
the right, entering another long hallway. They walked past
closed door after closed door, accompanied only by the
whistling wind and the shush of their footsteps on thick carpet. It did not occur to Hyacinth to count the doors they
passed until there had been too many to guess. The hallway
went on and on.

Finally, Mrs. Carter pushed a door open. She walked in
as if undisturbed by the thick darkness. For someone who
already knew the layout of the bedroom, the light of her flickering candle must have been sufficient to see what she needed.
Hyacinth's eyes followed the flame, but the light seemed to
only emphasize the surrounding darkness. Mrs. Carter moved
deeper into the room, then touched the candle flame to an oil
lamp on a small table. The room was slowly revealed by the
dim glow, and the housekeeper broke her silence.

"You may settle here. I'll bring up the rest of your bags."
She reached for the ring of keys at her waist and unfastened
one. "This is for your door. Be certain to lock it when you're
sleeping, and any time you're out."

Hyacinth thought the woman's instructions exaggerated
any possible danger in a near-empty building but said nothing
in reply. Mrs. Carter turned to the door, candle in her hand.

"Shall I help you?" Hyacinth asked.

With another glance from beneath that stern brow, Mrs.
Carter shook her head and stepped out the door.

"Thank you," Hyacinth said to the woman's retreating
back. She did not hurry to lock the door behind the housekeeper. The woman's warnings would not frighten her.

If Hyacinth had entertained a wish of finding the house-keeper to be a friend or a mother figure, someone with whom to share thoughts and feelings and tea, she knew it was time to reconsider. Dropping her cases to the floor, she kept Eleanor the orchid tucked in her arm as she stepped to the desk and lifted the lamp. Holding it high, she could nearly make out the corners of the room, the tall ceiling, the draperies surrounding the large bed, windows, a clothing cabinet along one wall, and a painting that might have been a garden of wildflowers, but she would study it more when the sun rose.

The room, though cold, was far more than satisfactory. It was lovely. Elegant. She drew close to the bed and used the lamp to inspect the pile of embroidered pillows. She tilted her head toward the orchid in her arm.

"Eleanor, I can hardly wait to climb into this nest and stay for hours."

A squeaking of door hinges surprised Hyacinth. Surely the housekeeper could not have made it down to the kitchen and back with her bags so quickly? She turned, but instead of Mrs. Carter's dark dress, she saw a flutter of white at the bedroom door.

There, and then gone.

A ghost? So soon upon her arrival? She felt nothing of the fear James had hoped to inspire; rather a shiver of satisfaction ran down her spine. This was more than she had hoped for. She wondered if the spirits of the house always moved so quickly to inspect a newcomer. She was certain that, were she a ghost, such a quick glance would not satisfy her curiosity.

She tucked Eleanor deeper into the crook of her arm. "How exciting," she whispered to the orchid.

A few steps brought Hyacinth to the door. The darkness of the vast hallway made the glow of her lamp useless to see far, but she tiptoed along the corridor back toward the huge staircase. Once or twice, she thought she could see a flicker of something white ahead, but never with enough clarity to be certain. Approaching the great curved stairway, Hyacinth slowed. Although she could see the other half of the house from the top of the stairs, it was accessible only by going downstairs to the entry hall and coming up the opposite staircase. She thought a light flickered down the hall on the other side, but before she could take more than a step toward the stairs, a door slammed, and the glow disappeared.

Despite the prickle of apprehension at the back of her neck, Hyacinth crept forward, moving slowly and softly. She only had the glow of her own lamp, which blinded her to anything more than a few feet away. Should she make her way down to the entry hall and back up the other side?

A shriek of wind brought her up short. What a terrible cry! She hesitated at the top of the staircase with her heartbeat thudding in her ears, unsure whether she wanted to hear the sound again to be assured that it was, in fact, the wind. For it would not take much to convince her the scream came from a pained human throat.

Something touched her from behind, and with a shriek of her own, Hyacinth's arms flew upward in defense. The lamplight juddered with the movement, but Hyacinth almost didn't notice. Her whole attention was fixed on her beloved orchid, which flew past Mrs. Carter's outstretched arm, and Hyacinth watched in horror as it crashed onto the staircase, tumbling down into the darkness.

LAMENT

Where can I find peace?

Do I not deserve solace and rest after the life I have suffered?

But no, perhaps I do not.

My mistakes marked me.

Penalties followed me here, and I bear the scars of my foolishness.

CHAPTER 3

Mrs. Carter's stern expression encouraged Hyacinth to keep her emotion in check. She should not cry in front of the housekeeper. She would not. Nothing in their interactions so far had given Hyacinth reason to suppose Mrs. Carter would be particularly gentle.

Of course, the woman need not possess a sympathetic nature to be effective at her work, and she might be a very qualified housekeeper. But at this moment, Hyacinth wished for a word of kindness. Mrs. Carter couldn't know that Eleanor was one of Hyacinth's late mother's favorite orchids. Even if she understood, the connection might not make sense to her. Hyacinth found few people who truly understood kinship with a plant.

She scrambled down the steps of the great curving staircase to find Eleanor's blue clay pot in pieces on the parquet floor. In the sputtering light of her lamp, she saw that the damage to the orchid was serious—crushed petals and folded leaves—but not severe. There was a good chance that, with significant caution and at least as much luck, she could save Eleanor.

Placing the lamp on the floor, Hyacinth whispered comfort to the orchid as she tucked the rhizome and the aerial roots into the front of her skirt, holding the stem below the lead bulb. Some of the petals had been torn off by the orchid's fall, but most remained intact; there was certainly room for hope.

Cradling the wounded Eleanor in her skirts, Hyacinth left the lamp on the floor and walked back up the steps to find Mrs. Carter still standing at the top of the grand staircase, the handles of Hyacinth's bags in her grasp. The housekeeper's face, lit by her own lamp, held strange shadows, making it hard for Hyacinth to determine the meaning behind her expression.

The two of them stood watching each other. What felt like several minutes seemed to stretch into forever.

Hyacinth knew she could not stand in awkward silence for another second, but when she spoke, her voice made almost no sound. She cleared her throat and attempted words again. "I tried to gather as much as I could of the mess. I apologize for any extra work I've caused you. After I place this back in my room, I will go back for the lamp."

With a sigh that made her lamplight flicker, Mrs. Carter said, "It's my fault. I apologize for frightening you. Here, take my light. I'll go after the other lamp and see that no shards from the pot are left to be stepped on."

Hyacinth saw real care and concern in the housekeeper's eyes. She wondered if this moment of gentleness was an aberration, or if the coldness of her reception was a pretense. Or maybe both were true, and Mrs. Carter was a more complicated character than Hyacinth initially assumed.

Mrs. Carter tucked her lamp into the crook of Hyacinth's arm with a gentle pat, which caused Hyacinth's breath to catch. This small and unexpected act of sympathy brought to the surface all the emotion she was trying to hide. She nodded and started down the hall toward her bedroom.

"Another moment, Miss Bell," Mrs. Carter said.

Hyacinth turned back.

Any hint of warmth was gone from the housekeeper's tone as she said, "You may be curious to enter hallways and explore parts of the house that are closed to you. I recommend that you resist such temptation. I cannot guarantee your safety if you cross the bounds of your own spaces."

Hyacinth stared. "Closed to me?" she echoed. "Safety?"

With a single nod, the housekeeper said, "You will avoid all locked doors, of course. You will never enter the north wing of the house, as it is closed off. This includes the north wings on each of the two upper floors. Those are family rooms. There will be no need for you to enter any of them, as there is nothing within that pertains to your work. Many of the family's treasured belongings that they could not transport overseas are stored in the rooms. Such areas are not to be disturbed."

With a gesture to the darkened hallway across the manor, the housekeeper took another step in Hyacinth's direction. Hyacinth resisted the urge to move backward. She glanced over Mrs. Carter's shoulder but could see no hint of light behind the housekeeper's back. Whatever Hyacinth had been following had disappeared down the north hall without a trace.

The woman went on. "You shall not enter any of the

closed areas of the house. There are dangers in an empty hall-way, and as Mr. Whitbeck surely made clear, you will follow the rules of the house to the letter or risk being sent away."

"But I believe—" Hyacinth began, but Mrs. Carter inter-rupted, her presence suddenly looming large.

"Is there a particular detail you don't understand about the risk of being sent away, Miss Bell?"

Hyacinth swallowed and managed to shake her head. "No, Mrs. Carter. I understand."

The housekeeper nodded, and she stepped back, giving Hyacinth fractionally more breathing room.

"You are welcome in your bedroom, of course, and when your work is done, to the kitchen, the sitting rooms in the main floor's south wing, and, naturally, the garden structures. All other rooms are forbidden."

Forbidden. Such a menacing word. So threatening. So deliciously *intriguing*.

Hyacinth shook her head to dislodge the thought. She ought not to be so interested and tempted by what was dis-tinctly outside her boundaries. She ought not, but she was.

And if Mrs. Carter saw the headshake as agreement that she would never venture into the forbidden hallways, even better.

Neither of the women moved. Hyacinth's feet felt planted to the floor. She could outwait the housekeeper. As they stood in the darkness, Hyacinth flicked another glance across the manor to the north hallway. Again, she saw nothing. But she knew something was there. Or at least, she was almost sure something had been there.

As Mrs. Carter seemed similarly rooted to the floor,

Hyacinth finally turned and continued walking down the hall toward her room, the housekeeper's lamp in her hand and the woman's eyes on her back. Between rumbles of thunder, she could hear the woman's skirts swish as they walked without speaking. The hallway seemed to roll out in front of her for miles, but she finally reached the open door of her new bedroom.

"Let us get these bags inside," Mrs. Carter said.

Hyacinth led the way into the darkness.

"In the morning," the housekeeper said, her tone hard and cold like steel, "you will find breakfast in the kitchen. Then you may familiarize yourself with the garden structures and read the notes that Mr. Whitbeck and his orchid expert have left for you."

Did she mention Mr. Whitbeck's previous gardener to make Hyacinth feel small? Did Mrs. Carter imagine that Hyacinth did not understand her station as a temporary replacement?

Hyacinth wondered if she could somehow cultivate a situation where she could see the woman's kindness again, or at least her gentler side.

Hyacinth said, "That will be delightful. Thank you, Mrs. Carter." She was determined to be as polite as possible so the housekeeper wouldn't suspect her of too much curiosity about the house, and about who or what might be sharing it with them.

"Good night, then," Mrs. Carter said as she placed the last of the cases inside the door.

"Good night," Hyacinth repeated.

The housekeeper nodded and walked away.

With a last look into the dark hall, Hyacinth closed her bedroom door and pressed her back to it.

The room, while still as lovely as it had been half an hour before, now felt larger, darker at the edges, and somehow sinister. What awaited her in the corners? The thrill she'd felt at seeing mysterious flickers of light throughout the manor dulled within the confines of a single room. Hyacinth felt less intrigued by the mystery now, and more fearful.

Afraid of her own bedroom? That would never do. No reason to worry about what might be lurking in the dark shadows of the room. She could investigate them herself. She was, after all, a scientist.

"The trouble with exploring dark corners," Hyacinth explained to the reduced but still beautiful Eleanor, "is that in order to see into one clearly, you must put your back to the others."

With a sigh, she set the lamp on the table near the window and set about finding somewhere to place Eleanor's roots and stem to keep them protected until she could get the orchid into the warm, damp shelter of the best hothouse on the Cornish coast—which happened to be on the grounds outside her window. After discarding the idea of using the cup and pitcher of water on the table, as she might need them herself, Hyacinth fashioned a nest from a fichu her father's housekeeper insisted she bring. With great care, she twisted the scarf's fabric into a base for holding and protecting Eleanor's shaken, tender roots from any further damage.

Although she knew it wouldn't matter, she made sure Eleanor's stem rose upright instead of leaning down onto the table. "That's right, my girl. Keep your head up," she whispered as she positioned the damaged plant against the side of the pitcher. "We'll get you repotted in the morning. First thing. I'm sure Mr. Whitbeck's orchid house has a lovely home that will fit you perfectly."

Even with Eleanor safely nested, Hyacinth knew she would not sleep a second until she had put her nerves to rest. Picking up the lamp, she walked slowly around the perimeter of the room, holding the light up high to see the corners where the walls met the ceiling, which were soaring and elegant and edged with moldings of positively extravagant detail, and then low, inspecting the floorboards, the carpets, and the furnishings.

Opposite the room's gilt-framed mirror stood a hulking black cabinet, its lacquered face reflecting the lamplight. Is this where she ought to keep her clothing? She pulled on the brass knob, but the chest did not open. Rattling the handle, she felt no give. It was locked.

Why would Mrs. Carter assign her to a bedroom with locked cabinetry inside? With all the dozens of bedrooms along this hallway alone, surely Hyacinth could have a useable cupboard for her things. She blew out a breath of frustration.

Her window, a dark glass facing the night's storm, rattled in its frame within the thick stone slabs that surrounded every window in the enormous manor. She gave a passing thought to the stonemasons who must have spent thousands of hours crafting the window casings, a small detail in such a vast building, but one she appreciated both from within the large house and from the outside. The eyes of the home.

The thought of windows as eyes had never felt quite so

disquieting, so spine-tingling. For not until now had she ever felt watched. Resting her forehead against the glass, she heard, even over the rain and wind, the sound of the sea, waves crashing onto the cliffs that rose from the water. Eventually, Hyacinth covered the window with the draperies and turned back toward the bed and rest.

Weak morning light leaked into the room from the edges of the curtains, and Hyacinth sat up in bed. Stretching her arms above her head, she took in the room lit with early gray gloom. At least she assumed it was early. Perhaps she had slept hours into the day, and the unrelenting storm kept the Cornish countryside under a blanket of clouds. Slipping from the bed, her feet found cold stone, and she shivered. She hurried to step on a carpet. If it was late in the morning, the house had not warmed much yet.

Donning her work dress, she gathered her notebook and pencil and placed them in the large pocket tied around her waist. It had been one of her mother's, embroidered with blue cornflowers and thyme leaves. It was a comfort to wear something that had belonged to her. As her mother had been a tiny woman and Hyacinth considerably taller, she held dear those wardrobe items that did not depend on size.

She picked up Eleanor and cradled her gently.

As she made her way down the hall toward the main staircase, Hyacinth debated making a quick excursion along the north hallway. In a house as large as this, how likely was

Mrs. Carter to be in the very forbidden hallway Hyacinth was desperate to explore at the very moment she wanted to see it?

Luck was not with her, however, for as Hyacinth approached the stairs, she saw Mrs. Carter polishing the railing, her dusting cloth wrapped around her hand.

"Good morning, Miss Bell," Mrs. Carter said, her face expressionless, nodding her acknowledgment even as she continued her cleaning.

Glad to hear it was still morning, Hyacinth gave a small curtsy and said, "My room was very comfortable. Thank you for all the work you've done to make it so." She would offer as many compliments as it would take until the woman chose to like her. Even if the effort seemed useless, as it did now.

"Breakfast items are in the kitchen," Mrs. Carter reminded her, not bothering to turn away from her work.

"How very kind. Thank you." Hyacinth couldn't hear the tiniest hint of a grumble in her voice. *Good work*, she told herself as she went down the stairs.

Making her way to the kitchen, she passed open doors leading to a ballroom, a library, and several sitting rooms. Paintings, some of which seemed very good and others with rather terrifying subjects, hung in ornate frames. Perhaps Mr. Whitbeck was an art collector as well as an orchid enthusiast. In any case, Hyacinth was pleased to see that none of these rooms appeared off-limits; at least she could peek inside on her way to breakfast.

A small collection of covered plates and platters sat upon a buffet in the kitchen. The eggs had gone cold, and the bread felt rather crusty. Still, she covered a slice of bread with soft butter and took a bite. Delicious. She lifted a beautiful green apple from a bowl and placed it in her pocket.

With her hand and mouth both full of bread, she made her way through the kitchen's back door into the courtyard she'd crossed the night before. No rain fell now, but heavy clouds made a dramatic background for the gray stone façade of Ashthorne Hall. Hyacinth looked up, trying to determine which of the windows was hers, and was sure the last of the row must be it.

She made her way to the nearest garden structures: two glass greenhouses and a steam-heated hothouse. She explored the greenhouses quickly, showing Eleanor that most of the bedding trays stood empty in early autumn. The tables in these buildings would normally hold sprouting seedlings from late winter until the plants were ready to be put into the gardens in spring. Along the edges of the greenhouses stood fruit trees of exotic origin sure to please the palates of people with year-round tastes for oranges and lemons. There were also a few fruits trees Hyacinth did not recognize.

As she entered the orchid house, she exhaled a long, satisfied sigh.

"Here we are, Eleanor. Welcome to your new room."

For the first time, she felt the possibility of feeling at home at Ashthorne Hall. Rows and rows of tables filled with orchids greeted her. From the rafters hung several vining varieties, growing in cascades, just as she imagined they would spill from trunks and branches of trees in ancient forests in their countries of origin.

Hyacinth knew that in their native states, orchids would cling to trees, but not in a parasitic relationship. Orchids grew on tree trunks and limbs but did not suck away nutrients from their host plants. They drew critical nutrition from surrounding fungi. If she had permission to make vast, radical changes to Mr. Whitbeck's gardens, she would love to bring potted trees into the hothouse and affix some of the orchids to the most tropical trees in an attempt to replicate their natural habitats. That was not a decision she could make by herself, however. She was here to tend, not to innovate.

Perhaps someday when she had gardens of her own.

Hyacinth wiped her fingers on her work skirt and pulled her pencil and notebook from the pocket. With the occasional help of the stakes and signs placed around the bedding trays and plant pots, she recorded each variety on display, careful to note relative size, color, and health. She counted bulbs and flower spikes, drew sketches of each variety of leaf and bloom, and generally lost herself in the great, lovely, humid hothouse.

When she grew hungry, she ate the apple from her pocket. She'd filled page after page of her notebook when she finally looked up to realize that the weak overhead light had brightened. Fragile rays of sunlight leaked through breaks in the clouds, and each pane of the greenhouse seemed to catch and scatter the beams.

"I believe we shall get a hint of sun now, my friends," she said to the plants. "Just what we all need. Stretch up to it. We can't know how long it might last."

She took her own advice and tilted her face to the brighter light for a few moments, closing her eyes and feeling the warmth intensify and recede with the passing clouds.

Sooner than she liked, the clouds again thickened. Looking back at the filled pages of her notebook, she realized that, although she'd explored only a fraction of the hothouse and its occupants, she had likely spent hours. She wondered if Mrs. Carter expected her to come inside for meals, or if she ought to continue to fend for herself as she worked. Would the housekeeper resent Hyacinth if a few late berries or tomatoes went missing from the kitchen garden?

She stretched her arms and her back, taking in the greenhouse, when movement outside one of the glass walls caught her eye. A flutter of white, stark against the green of the trees behind it, slipped along a window.

Hyacinth stuffed her notebook and pencil back into her pocket and ran toward the greenhouse door. Running, however, proved difficult in the crowded building. Tables stood at angles, supporting the orchids as they grew, sometimes to great heights and more often across many feet of space. It was by no stretch a maze, but the rows of tables were irregular, and it took Hyacinth longer than she liked to get out of the greenhouse.

She reached the door and stepped out into the glowing afternoon light, a breeze lifting her hair. Hurrying around the building, she saw nothing that could explain the flutter of white she'd seen through the window. No linens drying on a line, no white blossoms on a late-blooming rosebush dancing in the wind. She had known there would be nothing. What she saw had been in motion, as if it had a destination. Someone or something had passed the window. Possibly even stood at the window for a moment to look in at Hyacinth.

Could it be the same figure she was sure she'd seen at the door of her room last night?

A shudder crossed her shoulders, either fear or excitement, Hyacinth couldn't tell. In their correspondence, Mr. Whitbeck had asked if she would be nervous about living in a mostly empty house, but he hadn't given any indication there was something she ought to fear. Was there indeed a ghost at Ashthorne Hall, as James and Mr. Gardner had hinted? Had Mr. Whitbeck seen what she now saw? Perhaps his reassignment to India was more than circumstances of governing. Maybe he'd asked to leave this estate.

What if the man had taken his household and escaped Ashthorne?

No matter if her supposition was fancy or the truth, the idea of such a thing delighted Hyacinth. What more could this adventure offer if, indeed, it included a haunting?

LAMENT

Hidden. Secret.
But never still.
My ruin and my shame keep me always concealed—
But always moving. I am not at rest.
I am nothing like what I used to be.
I cannot show myself.
The ruin I have become is painful, both for me and for everyone else.
How would it feel to raise a flawless face to the sun once again?

CHAPTER 4

A cool morning breeze tickled Hyacinth awake, ruffling the yellow bed hangings. Sunlight streamed through the open window, a hint of what a perfect autumn day might be like here in Cornwall.

She was delighted to notice the difference sunshine made to her waking mood as she breathed in the scents of grass and trees tickling her nose. What a relief to wake each day to smells of growth in the country as opposed to the city scents that rose from the streets of London, where she had spent some time each year when her father had business in Town.

Eager to begin the new day, one already shining with morning light, she slipped from the bed, shuddering as her feet hit the stone floor, which never seemed to warm. This would only get worse, she imagined, as winter approached and the weather turned chill.

She walked to the mirror and stared at the mess her hair had become in the night. As she brushed through the dark, tangled knots, her eyes kept wandering to the black chest standing against the opposite wall, its polished surface catching the light from the window and reflecting it back from its shiny lacquered finish.

She set down the brush and once again turned to the chest. What was it? A clothing storage? Then why was it locked? Or did it hold something more interesting? More sinister?

She ran her hands along the sides of the cabinet. It appeared to be affixed to the wall. Not a movable furnishing, then. Part of the room.

But a part that was locked to her. More forbidden spaces. Hyacinth shook her head.

If a hairpin couldn't get her inside the cabinet—and indeed, it could not, as she soon discovered—she must put it out of her mind.

Stepping into her blue gardening skirt, which she had altered from its origins as a fashionable gown with bustle and requisite yards and yards of cloth into a far more functional item of clothing, she gathered her field notebook and the previous days' sketches and placed them in her pocket. How any woman could bear to wear a dress without pockets would always be a mystery to Hyacinth.

Before leaving the room for the day, she pulled the bed-clothes into place and folded her nightdress over the chair. Living without a household staff might have some disadvantages, but Hyacinth did not mind keeping her own space neat and orderly. And she had no occasion for fancy dresses or elaborate hairstyles. Simplicity was growing more appealing every day, and she was happy to have no need for Mrs. Carter to spend time in her room.

Passing the small night table next to the bed, she saw a

single cornflower, one that must have been picked yesterday and delivered to her room. Had Mrs. Carter noticed the embroidery on her pocket? Or perhaps it was an unconnected kindness, and the housekeeper simply regretted yesterday's coldness. Either way, Hyacinth smiled as she examined its perfect bloom, its leaves, its stem, and wondered how she had not noticed it as she climbed into the bed last night.

Drawing the flower to her nose, she inhaled the subtle scent and hoped she might find time that evening to walk into the wood and discover where Mrs. Carter had found it. She should dearly love to round a corner on a forested path and discover a field of cornflowers pulsing with blue light, even this late in the season. She tucked the bloom behind her car.

In the day and two nights that she had been at Ashthorne Hall, she had seen little of Mrs. Carter, mainly because Hyacinth had spent yesterday's hours in the greenhouse tending the vast rows of plants. A day spent in the company of orchids? Hyacinth was in heaven.

Especially when her only option for human companionship was unfriendly and standoffish. Of course, it was possible Mrs. Carter's coldness was only an effect of nerves. Maybe she had seen what Hyacinth saw in the hallways and outside the outbuildings. Perhaps Ashthorne's ghost frightened Mrs. Carter.

On her way to the stairs, Hyacinth found herself stepping quickly down the long hallway of the upper floor of Ashthorne Hall's south wing. The broad stone hallway felt dark even in the bright morning light. Probably an effect of the closed doors on both sides. A breeze seemed to be blowing through the corridor, but it felt friendly rather than distressing, the way it had when accompanied by a storm's howl.

She could only imagine the eeriness of these halls in deep winter, long, dark hours spent miles away from Suttonsbury village, the manor hemmed in by woods and backed by a craggy hill leading to a cliff face and down to the sea. Hyacinth felt grateful to be here in early autumn when daylight lasted so much longer and then chided herself for being silly; nevertheless, she could not deny the shudder running down her back. Even in daylight, the memory of flitting white images filled her imagination.

The wide staircases descending from the second floor to the vast foyer had a completely different aspect in the sunshine. The deep crimson carpets running along the center of each step brightened in the cheery light. Beams streamed in through windows that had, for the past two days, only shown spatters of rain and buffeting trees. What a glorious difference the light made.

Hyacinth stood at the landing and gazed into the foyer below, a space filled with stone pillars, ancient suits of armor, and dreary paintings of long-dead lords of the manor and their disappointed-looking wives and children. There was even a portrait of the saddest-faced dog Hyacinth had ever seen. But even these gloomy decorations took on a new quality in the morning light. Then she turned and looked up, following the staircase to the upper floor and to a hallway narrower than the one in which she stood, with many doors, presumably all locked to her.

Not that a locked door would necessarily keep her out.

Not for long. Her skills were not limited to orchid care, after all.

The soaring ceiling of the entryway rose to the floor of the top story, where the rooms must belong to the live-in staff when such was present. Hyacinth knew there must be at least one secondary staircase, for in a manor as fine as Ashthorne, no maid would walk up the elegant main stairway with a basket of kindling to lay a fire, not to mention carrying a bucket with which to clean.

As was becoming her habit when she descended the steps to the vestibule, she stared across at the north wing staircase. She wondered what she might find if she chose to ignore Mrs. Carter's demand that Hyacinth stay away from that side of the house.

Her desire to explore her surroundings was dampened by the housekeeper's restrictions, but what really kept Hyacinth from wandering the north wing was inside the hothouse. Even the possibility of mystery couldn't compete with the manor's glorious collection of orchids. There was still so much to explore.

Alongside the dish of apples was a bowl of peaches and a small basket of bread covered with a linen cloth. Hyacinth tucked an apple in her pocket for later, helped herself to a lovely peach, and lifted out a small loaf of bread. When Mrs. Carter had asked her about her breakfast preferences, Hyacinth worried that the woman might be offended by her simple tastes, but Mrs. Carter had been perfectly understanding. Each morning Hyacinth found fruit and bread, a most portable and agreeable breakfast, helped by the fact that there was some for now, and some for later.

Exiting the manor house through the kitchen door, Hyacinth walked along the flagstone path that meandered past the kitchen gardens and into the small grove of beech trees separating the first of the outbuildings from the main house. From her bedroom window, she had seen the farther-flung garden structures and follies, but she had not yet had a chance to explore them, though she was sure she'd be delighted when the opportunity arose. The orchids' hothouse came into view at the turning of the path, more stunning to Hyacinth than any of the other buildings. Its glass panels glinted in the morning sunlight, giving it a glow that matched the warmth of its enclosed space.

Formal gardens covered much of the grounds, some filled with late-blooming roses, some with ornamentals, and one with an elegant hedge maze. But beyond these, the edges of the woods bristled with craggy boughs and unstructured verges. Hyacinth could not tell, at least not from a distance, if the wilder trees and bushes had been cultivated once, or if they had managed to grow wild in such inhospitable soil conditions.

She imagined that when Mr. Whitbeck was on the premises with his entire household, staff, and crews of gardeners, the forest beyond the formal grounds would have been carefully kept at bay, but as the family now resided on a tea plantation in India, this older forest crept, leaf by twig by shrub, nearer the buildings, creating a sense of wildness that appealed to Hyacinth. She could picture all sorts of interesting creatures hovering close to the edges of the forest, watching the house and its occupants. Such thoughts gave her a thrill even with the warm sun on her shoulders—albeit a different kind of thrill than the thought would have in the dark.

She turned and looked at Ashthorne Hall from a new angle, appreciating its roofline towering high above, the dark gray walls peering through layers of ivy. The stones of the manor itself glowed now with a subtle warmth Hyacinth had not seen on the previous stormy day. Rather than appearing solidly gray and black, the building's stones carried an undertone of gold. But even in full morning light, the house was still forbidding. Possibly because much of it was forbidden.

Now, the morning sky, clear and cloudless, contrasted beautifully with the often-gloomy stone of the manor, and Hyacinth thought that some houses were simply suited to tempestuous weather. These walls seemed to call for dark, swirling clouds to enfold them.

If Ashthorne Hall was meant for rainstorms, the hothouse was built for mornings precisely like this one. Each pane of glass seemed to welcome in the sun's rays, multiplying them and scattering light and warmth throughout the rows and rows of orchid tables.

Upon entry, she breathed in the warm, damp air and felt herself immediately at home. She went directly to the first pot on the end of the nearest table. Her efforts to replant and strengthen her treasured orchid, Eleanor, had already borne fruit. Not literal fruit, of course, but Hyacinth could see Eleanor's stem strengthening, and several of the petals had managed to hold fast to the plant even after its horrifying crash down the stairs. She whispered a greeting to Eleanor and wished her a glorious day.

"I missed you last night. Perhaps I should bring you back

inside with me when I'm finished working in the evenings. And now, it's time to get to work. Enjoy this sunshine, dearest. We have no promise it will happen again."

Drawing on her calfskin garden gloves, she went to the second row of tables and bent her head over the small pink orchid that had begun showing signs of withering roots.

"Hello, Claude," she said, addressing the orchid by the name she had given it. "Lovely morning."

One of the greatest privileges of working with Mr. Whitbeck's orchids all on her own was the freedom to speak to the flowers. She had no delusions that her conversation would ever be reciprocated, of course, but she loved to prattle at the plants as though they were her friends. If nothing else, a steady stream of chatter made her feel less isolated as she spent her days alone in the orchid house.

After trimming the end of Claude's root, she saw that the plant next to it seemed to have mold spots on the leaves, which might mean it was too far from the circulating air. With a running commentary to the orchids, Hyacinth pulled her leatherbound notebook from the pocket of her skirt and noted the time, the sunny weather, and the imperfections in the leaves, including a hasty but serviceable sketch of the spots as they appeared today.

If it turned out the spots disappeared on their own, she would not need to remove the plant from its place, but if the mold grew, a new location might be necessary.

She inspected some of the front bulbs, which would likely become blooms, and the back bulbs, the swellings that held the nutrients that fed the plants. Humming her pleasure, she let the orchids know her opinions on their growth.

"Overall, I believe we can take comfort in these changes. I expect you to carry on as you have done, and I am as eager as you are to see these little swellings turn into blossoms."

Her inspection complete, Hyacinth moved to the next table, where Dendrobium and Phalaenopsis cuttings grew in a dozen identical pots. With a small wooden dowel, she lifted a leaf and craned her neck downward to inspect the underside.

"Why, Gretchen, you've developed such a lovely vein pattern here," she said, and, holding her notebook and pencil a few inches from her eyes, bent at the waist and twisted to get a good look at the underside of the leaves. "You're so humble, darling. Don't be shy. Show us all this pretty leaf of yours."

Hyacinth finished her quick sketch and unfolded herself from her contortion, rolling her neck to unkink her muscles. "I assure you if I had leaves as lovely as those, I'd not hide them."

Turning to her next orchid, she let out a frightened squawk, as unladylike a sound as she had ever uttered. A man stood before her in the greenhouse. She took a startled step backward, putting some small distance between them, and her hands flew into the air, as though the flailing of her arms could cast a protective wall between herself and the intruder. The wooden dowel fell from her hand, and the man, unruffled and unhurried, lifted his own hand to catch it midair without taking his eyes from her.

The corners of his mouth lifted in a gentle smile. "Miss Bell?" he asked, and at his tender glance and his quiet voice, Hyacinth's fear melted into something far more agreeable. Her heart gave a strong and not unpleasant lurch.

She nodded and lowered her hands.

"I am terribly sorry to have startled you," he said, the same smile playing on his lips. "I meant only to introduce myself. I was away from the property when you arrived. But, please, do not let me interrupt your conversation." He gestured to the flowers on the tables.

Hyacinth laughed at herself, amusement turning her flood of fear into relief, and then into embarrassment. Who was this man who'd witnessed her silliness? She brushed her hands along the front of her skirt, hoping she did not look as much a mess as she felt.

What was she supposed to say to him?

"Mr. Whitbeck?" she asked, halting and unsure. This man was so young. So handsome. So not what she pictured when she was hired to take care of his orchids.

Now he laughed. "No. Oh, goodness no. He resides in India, as I believe you know. Why on earth would you think I'm Mr. Whitbeck?"

"You're standing in his greenhouse," she said.

Of course he couldn't be the lord of the manor. This man was near her own age, casual in his confidence and polite to the hired help. A handsome face, but surely not a noble one. Too much sincerity in his smile. There was not any visible haughtiness of station, and no air of superiority marred his looks. The clothing he wore, though clean and tidy, suggested work rather than leisure. He stood with a posture of confidence but not self-importance.

He laughed again. "A coincidence, I assure you. I'm Lucas Harding. I'm acting as the estate's caretaker while the Whitbeck family is overseas. I have been away seeing to some business for a few days. Now I am back. I shall stop speaking soon, if I can manage it." He shrugged and gave a rueful shake of his head, causing his dark hair to tumble across his handsome brow. "I tend to increase in both speed and volume of speech when I feel nervous."

He did not appear nervous to Hyacinth, but she felt a thrill at the possibility that her presence had shaken him. His chatter put her instantly at ease.

His grin reappeared, and Hyacinth felt a shiver of delight to see it. He had a very charming smile, made even more pleasant by the suggestion that she was the cause of it.

"You have my most sincere apologies for making you nervous, sir," Hyacinth said. "I assure you I had no such intention. Nor have I gone mad, which you would be forgiven for assuming after seeing my interactions with the flowers and plants. If my discussion with the orchids was strange to you, please trust that I believed myself to be alone with them."

He took a small step closer. "I would never knowingly invade your privacy by intruding on a confidential conversation, even with a flower. I shall never disclose what I overheard; on that you have my word." His hand rested on his heart, just above the top edge of his lovely, patterned waistcoat.

His eyes smiled, but she did not feel any mockery. Only friendly admiration.

"Mr. . . . Harding, was it?" Hyacinth said, surprised to feel her heart pounding in her chest.

"Lucas, if you please," he answered.

Oh, that smile.

She matched his smile with her own. "Lucas, then. I

thank you for your discretion. One's secrecy is of utmost importance in matters of floriculture." She closed the ever-diminishing gap between them and held out her hand. "Hyacinth Bell. It is a pleasure to meet you, sir."

"The pleasure is all mine."

She believed him. He could have said anything at all and, accompanied by that smile and those eyes, she would have believed him. Lucas Harding closed her gloved hand in his own, and somewhere between the press of his fingers, the tilt of his mouth, and the glow in his eyes, Hyacinth lost her heart completely.

"I came in to water the orchids," he said, lifting a can from the edge of the table and tilting it toward the nearest plant. "I usually make sure to do that every day. I hope they haven't suffered in my absence."

"No," she gasped, and she feared her voice was as sharp as it was loud.

He tilted the can away from the flowers and glanced at her with a playful look. "Oh, did you already water this one today?" he asked with a grin.

She reached to pull the pitcher from his grasp, spluttering more denials. Then she marked his smile. She thought he might be teasing her, but she had to be certain.

"Mr. Harding, are you joking?"

He replaced the watering can on the table and raised his hands in surrender. "You have discovered me. Have no fear for your flowers. My only instructions for the care of the orchid house were to ensure the brazier was functioning and to not water *any* of the plants under *any* circumstances. I believe I read that instruction in three separate places."

She felt her muscles relax a fraction.

He leaned in as if imparting a secret. "You may or may not know this, Miss Bell, but orchids are a bit temperamental and should never be overwatered."

Now she laughed along with him, a wave of gratitude that he had not been watering the orchids flooding through her. "I am aware of the intricacies of orchid care," she said.

Mixed in with amusement and relief, she noticed an increase of her own heartbeat, a flutter in her center. This strange reaction overwhelmed her as she observed each system's response. Her eyes turned toward his; her hands yearned to reach for him. Never before had she felt so immediate an attachment to any man, and she surprised herself with a confidence he might feel the same.

At the moment, though, she simply wanted to keep him close. She initiated more conversation so he would not feel the need to leave her to her work.

"Because you are the caretaker, sir, I would like to demonstrate the great delicacy with which I have been looking after Mr. Whitbeck's orchids." She turned and gestured ahead, and Lucas fell into step beside her as if they had been walking together for their whole lives.

"I would be grateful for the exploration," he replied, offering his arm.

How comfortably they passed from row to row, she showing him a swelling bud or a tilting leaf, he nodding and smiling as they went.

After several long moments that felt far too fleeting to Hyacinth, she asked him a question that ought to have occurred to her in the beginning. "Are you at all interested in orchids, Mr. Harding?"

He smiled at her. "Why do you ask? Have I not been attentive to your tour?"

"I mean no disrespect by mentioning this, sir, but as I showed you Mr. Whitbeck's priceless, prizewinning specimens, I am not at all sure you noticed them."

He shook his head. "I am sure they are remarkable."

She pressed her hand against his forearm and lowered her voice, leaning closer in confidence. "But you did not look."

With a smile shaded with remorse, he answered, "I fear I am guilty of being distracted. Please do not be offended when I tell you the flowers all look the same to me. I have seen the orchids before, but I have not had the pleasure of watching you at your work. Your expression as you explain the tiny differences you see in each plant is captivating."

Hyacinth's heart pounded all the way to the ends of her fingertips. *Goodness,* she thought. *What a lovely thing to say.*

Lucas Harding was not like the men Hyacinth had known in London. Though his manners were far less formal, they were far more pleasing. He did not seem to conform to parlor rules or ballroom expectations. In his jesting and playfulness, he was a great relief.

However, as no man had ever spoken to Hyacinth with such intensity, she did not know how to answer, and so said nothing. For a few seconds she watched the expression change in his face from amusement and admiration to a shuttered caution.

He took a half step away from her side, increasing the distance between them. "I ought not to have spoken so boldly. Nor should I stare so openly. I fear I am behaving with complete impropriety." He gave a visible effort to pull his eyes from her face. "Please forgive me. If you would care to continue the tour, I would love to hear more."

Hyacinth removed her hand from his arm and turned toward him. "The orchids are not likely to become any more fascinating." She gestured to the hothouse at large and watched the lightness return to his expression along with that smile.

With a grin of her own, she asked, "Perhaps we could delay the rest of the exploration and merely talk?"

Because people tended to be more complex than flowers, Hyacinth's reactions to introductory conversations bordered on unreliable. Cues could be misread, actions misinterpreted, but she was certain that Lucas Harding felt a surge of happiness at her words.

He beamed. "Shall we sit here?" he asked, gesturing to a grouping of chairs around a small table covered with a stack of Hyacinth's notebooks.

Lucas sat with his back to the whole of the orchid collection. She thought hers was as near to a perfect view as any she had seen.

"How do you find Ashthorne, Miss Bell? Is your situation all you might have expected in a position of employment?" he asked.

Hyacinth suspected he knew all about her employment arrangement with Mr. Whitbeck and assumed he simply wanted to hear her speak, which she was delighted to do.

"I have spent several years studying botany both at my father's estate in the country and in London." She watched to see if he would make a sign that he understood what a rare opportunity that was for a woman, even in these days of increasing opportunity and education. He did not seem shocked, and nodded as she continued her explanation. "It turns out I have a propensity for orchid care. When Mr. Whitbeck planned his move to India, I was recommended to him as someone who could come to Cornwall to care for his plants. As I was unattached, I agreed to move here and manage his orchids."

"Unattached?" Lucas repeated.

Hyacinth smiled at the direct—and indirect—question. Did drawing-room rules apply in the hothouse? Was she supposed to be coy? She knew very well what he was asking, but she did not mind if he worked a bit harder to say it.

She smiled. "Nothing kept me from accepting the employment."

"Nothing and no one?" he pressed. She did not resent any such emphasis.

"For several years now, I have been mistress of my own choices. My father trusts me with a generous freedom to make my life my own without objection," she answered, quite certain that Mr. Harding understood her clarification about her relationship status.

She could speak more boldly than some of society's more proper ladies would ever dare to, but even she could not simply look at a man she just met and say, "I am entirely available." The very thought made her blush.

She hurried on. "I have been delighted by this place." She gestured to the building in which they sat, surrounded by green and growing things, the scents and colors filling the hothouse with verdancy.

"The greenhouses and other garden structures?" he asked.

"All of it. The manor house is rather spectacular." She leaned closer. "If I'm honest it gives me chills, but I do not mind being frightened once in a while."

He looked concerned. "The house frightens you?"

"Not the house. The doors are sound, and Mrs. Carter is certainly capable of keeping us safe and unbothered, just as I am sure you are an excellent caretaker. No, my security here is assured. But the feeling of the manor itself?" She shook her head. "The hallways are so dreary, and the stones weep in wet weather. Drafts whistle so morosely in the night. When you take in the estate as a whole, with its windblown forests and rocky cliffs and rooms full of furniture draped in holland covers, it feels exactly like something out of a novel. It rather drips gloom. Add in that dreadful portrait gallery in the south wing, and the place really does seem ripe for a haunting." She grinned to show him she was being silly, but he had lost his smile.

Wanting to give him an opening in playful conversation, she asked, "Do you object to ghost stories, Mr. Harding?"

He inspected the fingers of his right hand. "They do not amuse me now as they used to when I was young."

"I believe you are still considered young in many circles," she said, hoping her jest would turn the tenor of the conversation back to something light and easy.

His response remained solemn. "It is many years since I felt like a young man, no matter how few years I've lived."

Had he suffered a tragedy?

She knew she could not ask.

Mr. Harding was silent, staring past her head at something or nothing.

That was not at all the turn Hyacinth was hoping for. But she could commiserate. "Several years ago, my mother died. I was blessed to have a doting and caring father, but even so, since her passing, I have felt a loss of the innocence and joy of childhood."

He looked at her directly and nodded. "I have suffered losses, as well."

"Your parents?" she asked, hoping she did not appear aggressive in her question.

He nodded again. "They died too young. And my dear cousin Rosa, in an unrelated tragedy. And now my only sister is ill."

He did not say more, and Hyacinth did not ask. Instead, she said, "Sadness sometimes follows me, but I find a great deal of pleasure when I attend the orchids. Something about being surrounded by growth and beauty and the unrepentant redundancy of bud after bud, bloom after bloom makes me very happy."

He smiled at her, all hints of his morose expression gone from his handsome face. "I am so glad you have come to Ashthorne to be happy, Miss Bell."

LAMENT

I see the way things change around me,
Without my permission,
As if the world has sped
To spin and turn twice as quickly
Since I walked away from that life—
From that death.
I can never keep up,
And I fear I'll never learn to understand.

CHAPTER 5

When Hyacinth could think of nothing more to say without resorting to listing his charms, she decided to invite a change of scenery. After all, would Mr. Harding be interested in hearing that she thought him witty and handsome and attentive?

She asked, "Mr. Harding, would you show me about the grounds? I have seen very little beyond what I pass when I walk from the kitchen door to this hothouse. I would love to see the property through the lens of your experiences here."

Was that far too forward a suggestion? It seemed not, as Lucas Harding moved quickly from his seat and held out his hand to her, his eyes never leaving hers.

"I'm rather an expert on the shoreline, if you'd agree to a walk along the beach." When he smiled at her like that, wide and welcoming, she was confident she'd follow him anywhere.

"Is there a beach, then?" she asked, putting her hand in his. "I hear waves crashing upon rocks from my window at night, but when I looked, it was only water and cliff."

She was surprised that his touch did not carry her away

from reality completely, the way some of her friends spoke of losing their senses at the touch of a handsome and charming man. Instead, Hyacinth felt more firmly aware of her fingers where they touched him, of her thoughts, of her surroundings. It was as though this small connection to Lucas Harding made the entire world more clear.

"There is a line of sand which appears only at low tide."

"Then the pirates must plan their attacks by the tides," she said.

"Pirates?" he asked. "Do you know something I don't?"

Possibly a great many things, she thought, *that I would be happy to share.* But instead of answering, she shook her head. "Do you know Mr. Gardner in the village?" At his nod, she continued. "He warned me about all sorts of things that go on up this way. Pirates are only the beginning. Ghosts, too. Possibly ghosts of pirates."

He laughed and led her out of the hothouse. "And his tales have not scared you away yet?"

She grinned. "Perhaps in time. Given enough pirates and specters, even the strongest of us might begin to shudder and faint."

"I don't believe you are the fainting type," he said. The way he watched her, with an open expression of delight in her conversation and a sparkle in his deep brown eyes, gave her a thrill.

As they turned along a gravel walk leading behind the house, she asked him, "Did your family always live here at Ashthorne?"

When he shook his head, his hair curved over his brow, giving him at once an air of heroism and childlike innocence.

She resisted the urge to reach up and sweep the unruly lock back into place.

"I spent my childhood years in Suttonsbury village, before my parents passed. My father owned and farmed a small plot of land, and after he died, I sold it off to pay for schooling. I came to Ashthorne after my aunt Ellen—that is, Mrs. Carter—learned that Mr. Whitbeck would be leaving the manor."

"Oh," Hyacinth said. She schooled her features so her expression wouldn't give away her surprise. "Mrs. Carter is your aunt?" She felt glad she had not begun this conversation by asking if the housekeeper was always in a foul mood.

Lucas nodded and gave a gentler, calmer version of his smile, one that curled up on the left and showed only a few of his strong, straight teeth.

He continued. "She did not want to stay here alone, and so she secured this position for me. I live in the caretaker's cottage just over the path." He gestured back along the footpath that Hyacinth had walked many times, though she had never noticed a building that appeared to be a dwelling.

She wondered if it lay beyond her traveled track or perhaps deeper in the trees. But now that she knew such an interesting person lived nearby, she thought it worth the effort to be a good neighbor. Not that she would be so bold as to drop in on him uninvited or alone. But the idea of sitting with him in a cozy cottage did have its charms.

"And your sister?" she asked.

"She lived in Suttonsbury for a time," he said, but he offered no more about her. The sound of the surf grew louder, and his voice rose with it. "And you? Brothers? Sisters?"

She would show him the proper way to answer such a question. "I have an elder brother and an elder sister, both of whom have married and settled in homes far from our family estate. My brother and his wife have two pernicious children, wicked enough to convince anyone that the only logical solution is to lock them up in an attic until they reach their majority. I adore them both beyond measure and visit as often as they will have me."

She was delighted at his laugh. Oh, she dearly hoped she could make him laugh again.

Lucas gestured with his arm as they rounded a curve, and the sea came suddenly into view. A half-moon cove sparkled beneath them in the afternoon sunlight. As they approached the edge of the cliff, Hyacinth looked down and drew in her breath. It was thirty feet or more from this spot to the water and the line of sand bordering it. They stood for a moment staring at the sea, and Hyacinth's heart pounded. Whether from the majesty of the shoreline or the nearness of Mr. Harding, she was not willing to guess.

She went on, circling back to his question about her family. "My sister is a beauty and a wit. She never had much use for me, which might be a result of the many times I'd let myself into her locked room with the help of stolen keys and dozens of ruined hairpins. It's possible some of her good drawing pencils and bottles of perfume went missing."

Lucas delighted her with a look of shock. "You were a robber?" he asked, a hand to his chest in mock horror.

She tilted her head. "There is debate about that. Did I rob? Or did I merely steal? It hardly matters now, since we both refuse to think of it anymore. She, because I rarely cross her mind. Me, because I refuse to dwell on my childhood evils. She was a great success in her season and continues to charm and delight London society each summer. She and her husband host dinners and card parties." Hyacinth gave Lucas a pointed look, hoping he would understand her position on both dinners and card parties.

He seemed to sense the change in her tone.

"Do they not include you?" he asked, his voice gentle. He adjusted his arm around hers to cup her elbow in support as they descended the path cut into the stone along the cliffside.

"I am sure they would welcome me, but London society does not agree with me. I prefer gardens to balls. Perhaps I can convince my sister and her husband to build a hothouse like Mr. Whitbeck's on their estate in Herefordshire, and then I could tend the flowers she uses to decorate her dinner table." Hyacinth couldn't hide the hint of longing in her voice that her sister would value her, even though Hyacinth was quite pleased with how her own life was turning out.

"And your parents?" he asked.

"My father and my mother found great comfort at home. My brother and sister were already grown and gone when my mother passed, so my father made me his companion. I worked next to him as he studied, and I learned by watching him. When I wanted to study botany in my own right, he arranged for me to train with some of England's preeminent scholars. He is completely supportive. He misses me when I am gone; he is visiting Provence this autumn to avoid the loneliness."

"I cannot imagine anything filling the void when you leave," he said, his voice soft and low and deeply penetrating to Hyacinth's heart. His warm smile gentled to a soft look, one that spoke comfort and certainty.

The gaze they shared sank deep into Hyacinth's heart, and she wondered at the turn of events that had brought her to this day, this manor, and this position. Her whole life seemed to be blessed, and she felt her fortune.

She did not know the proper way to reply to such a comment and the serious feeling that followed, so she made it a jest. "You, sir, have known me for less than an hour. I assure you, years of association tarnishes some of my immediate charms."

Smiling, he shook his head. "I rather doubt it."

His conversation tended so readily to the gentle compliment. She had never spoken with a man who flirted with such ease and sincerity.

Wanting to avoid gaping at him, she turned the topic to his work. "What is it you do as caretaker of Ashthorne Hall?"

He answered very slowly, with a distinct pause between each word. "I take care."

She laughed. "Surely the stones in the walls would crumble without your superintendence. What precisely do you care for? Have you had to chase away bandits?"

"No bandits as of yet," he said. "But I assure you, I am prepared to give chase."

He gestured at the path, and she nimbly stepped over a stone in their way.

She nodded. "I feel more confident knowing of your readiness. What else?"

"In the summer, I found hedgehogs in the chicken roost."

"Imagine mistaking one for an egg," she said.

Lucas rubbed his fingers. "I don't have to imagine," he said, his face mock-mournful. "I remember it clearly."

"And aside from displacing hedgehogs and preparing to pursue highwaymen?"

He shook his head. "Nothing terribly interesting. If a tree falls, I cut it up. If a neighbor's cow moves into our fields, I move it back out again. When Ellen needs supplies, I drive a wagon to the village for her."

She understood he was downplaying his role at the estate, but she did not press. She was beginning to recognize his humility, and it only added to his other more visible charms. She decided to wait for him to answer more fully, and if he chose to say no more, she would simply watch him as they walked down the narrow cliffside path. And given his broad shoulders and narrow waist, she did not mind that option.

"The real work will begin when the family decides to come back," he said, turning the subject away from himself. Perhaps he had grown uncomfortable under her gaze. "Until then, I simply maintain."

Hyacinth did not have any interest in discussing the return of the Whitbeck family, for when they left the tea plantation, they would bring their current orchid specialist back with them, along with all the new specimens he gathered while in India. There would be no place for her here then.

"I imagine there is always something that needs starting or finishing or replacing or repairing." She knew she was speaking too much, but the way Lucas locked his eyes on her, that look of delighted wonder upon his face—as though he were the most fortunate man in the world—rather took her breath and stole her concentration.

He pointed to the right, and they stepped off the stone path onto a stretch of sand. The tall cliff walls formed a crescent, and toward the horizon, the sea sighed and breathed. Hyacinth took in the beautiful view, knowing that the inherent dangers of the landscape and the water added to its wonder. She felt the surface of the sand shift beneath her shoes.

"How high does the water go?" she asked, looking up at the cliffs beside them.

He pointed. "Tides are highest at this time of year. Especially during autumn's full moons. See these holes in the stone? If you stand up there at the tip of the crescent, you'll see many of the holes are covered by water at high tide. Now, and most often during a storm, the water is treacherous. I hope you won't come down here and walk this way alone."

She looked up at him. "I'd much rather come with you," she said, and felt her cheeks warm at his returning smile.

"Often my work consists of long walks like this upon the grounds." He looked at his shoes and then back at Hyacinth. "I hope you can join me again on occasion. And I might be persuaded to open the ancient, crumbling chapel if you promise only to go there with the protection of my company."

"Am I so easy to read? Is it obvious that I'm a person who would adore a crumbling chapel?" she teased.

"You seem to be ready and willing to be pleased by whatever Ashthorne shows you."

She wanted to say that she was pleased by whatever *he* showed her, but she chose to keep that to herself.

"You mentioned protection. Do you fear for my safety in a church?" she asked, smiling.

"Not any more than I fear for your safety on the beach at low tide. No, not fear, exactly, but your welfare is a concern of mine now."

Did she imagine his gaze grew more intense?

He seemed to recollect himself and hurried to explain. "Because you are a member of Ashthorne's staff and a resident of the house, I mean. I am tasked to prevent trouble here, so your safety is paramount. I would go to great lengths to assure it."

She answered him with a smile. She had never fallen into such easy intimacy with any man. He captured her in his gaze and made her feel precious and protected. What may have been several long minutes passed without a word from either of them as they contemplated each other, and she basked in the good fortune of the moment.

She looked out to sea. "It's lovely here."

He nodded. "Lovely and perilous."

"Why is it that those two things so often go together?"

He did not answer. After a moment, he turned them back toward the upward path.

As she kept pace with him, she asked him another question. "You mentioned you have been traveling," she reminded him. "Did you visit someplace pleasant?"

"London," he said. "I was sent to visit a doctor."

"Are you unwell?" she asked, realizing too late that her question was perhaps too familiar.

"On behalf of my sister," he said. "Do you know London well?"

He was sidestepping her questions, but she allowed herself to be led into a different topic, happy to be in even a superficial conversation about the most common delights of the city. She would have gladly gone back to hedgehogs in the henhouse as long as they continued to speak together.

Hyacinth barely noticed the sun's movement across the sky, so delighted was she with spending the afternoon in Mr. Harding's company.

After climbing back to the cliff top, they explored one of the estate's follies—buildings separate from the manor's main structures, built for entertainment and beauty. Inessential and charming, they struck Hyacinth as delightful. She and Lucas climbed the rise to the hill to view Ashthorne Hall from partway up the rise at the back of the extensive property. Hyacinth said, "This is a remarkable estate. We might spend hours more and never see all of it."

At her mention of hours, Mr. Harding made an apology. "Miss Bell, I fear I have kept you far too long. Surely you are famished."

"I believe I shall survive my current hunger, but in an effort to monopolize every minute of your day, I would like to invite you to join me in the house for tea." She straightened her dirty gardening skirt as if a tug here and there would make her presentable for a meal in shared company in any room within the manor house. "But as I have not been making preparations for any such tea, we shall be entirely at Mrs. Carter's mercy as far as both food and drink are concerned. We can stop in the kitchen garden and filch some beets, perhaps."

He smiled and brought Hyacinth closer into his side. "I believe Ellen can improve upon the beet plan. Her position as housekeeper does not stop her from stepping into any other role in the household, particularly when the household is just us."

"She is your aunt, I believe you said?" She remembered him telling her about his connection to the housekeeper, but she would lead him into more familiar conversation any way she could. Hyacinth kept her hand in the bend of his elbow as they moved along the path to the manor.

"Yes. She's my mother's youngest sister. We have been close for many years, but most especially since her only daughter passed away."

Hyacinth spoke quickly to cover her discomfort at introducing a topic that might bring him pain. "Oh, I'm terribly sorry. This is the cousin you spoke of—Rosa? Was it an accident?"

"An illness," he answered, in the short response that Hyacinth was learning marked the end of the topic.

"Mrs. Carter is good at her job," Hyacinth said, eager to steer the conversation to a less tender topic. "But she seems rather strict. Intent about the rules."

He seemed not to hear the second part, but he nodded and agreed to the first. "She always has been very kind," he said, and then, with a smile of renewed brightness, "and she is always happy to cook for me."

"Which is reason enough to love someone," Hyacinth teased.

As they approached the manor, she was delighted that Lucas kept her hand on his arm. Entering the house through the kitchen door, they discovered Mrs. Carter slicing cold beef and placing it on a platter beside a pewter dish full of late-season strawberries.

She looked up from her work, and then glanced at their entwined arms. Hyacinth stiffened in readiness for a reprimand for being in such a familiar posture.

She had no need for such worry.

"Ah, Lucas. You've met our guest," Mrs. Carter said with a smile. "If you two could see your way to the blue drawing room, I will bring a platter of food in directly."

Hyacinth was half confused by the closeness of Lucas Harding and half afraid Mrs. Carter might change her mind and shout at her.

"As I am not truly a guest, there is no need for any kind of formality," Hyacinth said. "I am sure we would be perfectly happy to stay in the kitchen."

Mrs. Carter glanced at Lucas and said, "What is the use of having the run of a place like this if we do not use it? I shall join you momentarily."

Her voice, her looks, and her actions were so much kinder now that Lucas was present. Perhaps Mrs. Carter was afraid to be alone in the manor when he was away. Surely she had seen the ghostly flickers in the night. Ashthorne's halls and passages were so dark and could feel quite confining, and with only a strange botanist in residence, she must have been feeling a very natural gloom. Hyacinth recognized that gloom, and she knew that to someone without her adventurous outlook, such a thing might appear frightening indeed.

In any case, she was glad to see Lucas made Mrs. Carter smile.

She understood the reaction perfectly. She was fighting a constant smile herself.

Lucas led Hyacinth into the blue drawing room, named,

she had to assume, for the damask draperies and the painted ceiling. He led her to a chair, which she took, carefully arranging her skirts so as not to dirty the furniture. She debated excusing herself to change her clothes, but Mrs. Carter would arrive soon, and Hyacinth did not want to ask the housekeeper to wait.

She noticed a painting hanging between two windows. "Is this a view from the house? It looks somewhat like the hill we climbed this afternoon."

"I assume you mean the *mountain*," Lucas said with a grin. "The Whitbeck family is excessively fond of their mountain, and there are images of it throughout the manor."

"Are there? Perhaps you could show them to me," she said.

As though a fog blew in, his countenance clouded. Just as quickly, his smile returned. "We can make a study through the open rooms of the south wing in search of reproductions of the hill."

"The mountain," Hyacinth said, a false sternness in her voice.

"Naturally," he replied. "In the meantime, you ought to examine some of the paintings that give this room its name."

Hyacinth pointed to the blue draperies with eyebrows raised in silent question.

"Common misconception," he said, nodding. "But the window coverings came after the name. This room is called the blue drawing room because, with the exception of the mountain there, each painting on these walls is a study in sadness. Not a cheerful expression to be found. Only gloom and dismay and disappointment."

"You are teasing," she said, standing up and moving toward the near wall.

He placed a hand to his heart. "I give you my word, my lady. The room is even more blue in mood than in color."

They circled the drawing room, stopping before each painting.

"You may be right," Hyacinth said, pointing out the boy and girl standing by a small stone bench. "Those are the sullenest children ever painted."

"I warned you," he said with a smile.

"This one is rather pretty," Hyacinth said, pointing to a landscape.

He shook his head. "Weeping willow," he said. "Tragic."

"Are you a specialist in the blue drawing room only, or do you have this level of expertise throughout Ashthorne?"

"I would not like to brag," he said with a wink, suggesting he would, in fact, love to brag, "but a good caretaker must know his property inside and out."

"And you are a good caretaker?" she prompted.

"Have you ever met a better one?" he asked in return.

At what point did she again take his arm? When did he lean closer so their heads nearly touched? For how long had the length of his leg been hidden by a fold of her skirt? When Hyacinth felt a pang of hunger, she realized that Mrs. Carter was still not in the room. Had she looked in, seen them in this familiar attitude, and turned away, unwilling to intrude?

Hyacinth wondered if she ought to ask Lucas. Would he be shocked or offended at the suggestion that their attentions to each other were too bold, particularly so early in their acquaintance?

Before Hyacinth could formulate a question, Mrs. Carter stepped into the drawing room. She looked ruffled and upset, her cheeks flushed and hair mussed. She had a streak of something upon her face as well as on her apron.

Hyacinth dropped Lucas's arm and went to the housekeeper. "Are you hurt?"

Mrs. Carter forced a laugh. "Hurt? Of course not, Miss Bell. I am perfectly well. Do sit down and take your tea," she said, attempting a tone of unconcern.

Hyacinth did not believe the tone for a second. But, unwilling to press the housekeeper, she seated herself. Lucas took the tray from Mrs. Carter, leaning close and whispering something Hyacinth could not hear. She tried to hide her surprise at this blatant act of secrecy in her presence.

After a whispered reply, Mrs. Carter chuckled again, this time with a touch more assurance. "A chicken got into the kitchen," she said. "Goodness, try to say that quickly. A chicken in the kitchen. I had to chase it out again before it caused a tremendous mess."

Whatever Mrs. Carter had been doing, Hyacinth doubted it involved poultry. But the woman was clearly flustered, so Hyacinth chose to play the part of the gracious guest as Mrs. Carter and Lucas moved awkwardly around each other in their efforts to serve tea.

A slice of cold beef and a savory scone helped take the edge off Hyacinth's fierce hunger, but she eyed the tray, hoping for a bowl of the lovely strawberries she had seen in the kitchen.

Mrs. Carter saw her glance. "Can I offer you more, Miss Bell?"

"This is delicious, thank you. I only wondered if you had brought in the berries from the kitchen."

Another look passed between Lucas and Mrs. Carter, his questioning, hers flustered. Lucas barely shook his head, and Mrs. Carter smiled falteringly at Hyacinth. "Isn't that the mess of it? That was the very thing the rogue chicken wanted. Came in and pecked through the lot of them. Had to throw them all out, and they were the last of the ripe strawberries in the garden. I shall look for some more later in the week." She looked around the room as she spoke, as if Hyacinth was making her nervous.

"Meantime, this scone is delicious," Lucas said, helping himself to a second and then offering the tray to Hyacinth. "Aunt Ellen has always made the best scones."

Mrs. Carter sat in front of the window and tucked her chin demurely, murmuring in reply.

Hyacinth swallowed a bite of her scone. "Mr. Harding tells me that the two of you are good friends as well as relations," she said, hoping to help Mrs. Carter regain her composure. "And that you have been very kind to him."

"Any kindness on my part is amply repaid by himself," Mrs. Carter said, patting Lucas on the knee. "We all do our best to care for each other," she said with a smile that finally approached her former one.

"All?" Hyacinth echoed.

"We two," Mrs. Carter said, furrowing her brow and exchanging another glance with Mr. Harding.

Something had changed. The mood of the room had moved from light to secretive. Mrs. Carter, who fluctuated between cold and welcoming, held a secret she did not want

Hyacinth to know. And Lucas Harding knew that secret. He laughed with Hyacinth, and then he murmured with Mrs. Carter. They kept her out of their conversation. Perhaps this was a hint that Hyacinth ought to keep to herself at Ashthorne, to tend the orchids and join the others for tea and take herself to her bedroom.

But she could not deny the attraction she felt toward Lucas, the immediate comfort she experienced when she was with him. His smile lit her up like a flare. No, it was too late for her to decide to have nothing to do with Lucas Harding.

Hyacinth wondered what in the world was being masked behind those smiles. What did the two of them discuss that could only be said in whispered voices?

After a few more minutes, tea drew to a close, and Mrs. Carter began to clear the food away.

Lucas stood and said, "Please let me."

She patted his arm. "Oh, I think your time would be better served showing Miss Bell some of the principal rooms. Off with you, now."

LAMENT

Is it so much to ask to be allowed a friend?
But no.
There are rules.
I know the house is not mine
And I have no right to demand who goes where.
But every day, every hour I wish
For companionship.
Someone like me.
But I know the truth—there is no one like me.

CHAPTER 6

On the arm of Lucas Harding, Hyacinth felt far fewer terrors in Ashthorne Hall than she had during the last two dark nights of rain and wind. In fact, as they kept to the main floor of the south wing, exploring parlors and sitting rooms and a ballroom, their walk through the manor left Hyacinth feeling warm toward the building and all its inhabitants, real and imaginary, current and former, pleasant and irritable, mortal and supernatural.

The manor's grand ballroom, a vast square with chandeliers lowered on their chains from the soaring ceilings and draped in white cloth, gave Hyacinth a delicious thrill of both terror and anticipation. Terror because the fabric, tickled by the seemingly ever-present breaths of wind, flitted and flickered like ghosts, especially when she caught the movement from the corner of her eye and just out of her focus.

And the anticipation? Might there be a reason, an excuse to dance here someday with Mr. Lucas Harding? Her logical mind knew that her two sets of gardening skirts, her travel costume, and her serviceable but not stylish dinner dress would hardly make her a fashionable addition to any party, even on the slim chance more than three people gathered to share a meal in Ashthorne Hall.

Oh, but her imagination supplied plenty of spinning and glancing and hand touching. How strange, she thought. She had never felt like this before. Was the house making her silly? Or was it Lucas himself?

She glanced at his face.

If he entertained thoughts of holding Hyacinth in his arms for a tender Viennese waltz or cheery Bohemian polka, his outward expression did not change. He maintained a pleasant and gentlemanly demeanor throughout their stroll.

Lucas showed her the silk wall-coverings in the morning room, and she amused herself for a moment trying to see where the fabric was seamed. Could silk be woven as wide as a whole room?

As they walked into the next room, Hyacinth gasped. "Is that a harp?" She pointed to a tall shape covered with a cloth standing on a pedestal next to a likewise cloth-draped piano.

"Do you play, Miss Bell?" His question might have been an excuse to say her name. She did not mind in the least.

"No, but if it's not a harp, I should surely not like to find myself in this room after dark. The white gauzy fabric would terrify me, looming as it does."

She laughed at herself, but he became serious again. "I hope you won't roam through the manor in the dark."

She smiled at the floor. "No. No, of course not."

What Lucas Harding did not know need not keep him awake at night.

"Do you play?" she asked him, hoping to nudge his attention away from any thought of her forbidden nocturnal wanderings.

"Not the harp, no." His answer seemed to hold an opening for another question.

She pointed to the other covered instrument. "The piano, then? Do you know how to play that?"

He ducked his head. "Our family had a rather grubby little spinet, and I loved to play."

Hyacinth made a sound of encouragement, and he went on, now with more confidence. "My sister and I would make up new words to the hymns we sang in church. We would sit side by side on the little piano stool and play duets, laughing until one of us fell from the seat."

She loved seeing another layer of this man's personality, discovering more to like with every moment they spent together. "Would you play for me?" she asked.

Lucas Harding stepped to the side of the large and elegant piano and smiled as widely as she'd seen yet. She felt that smile warm every part of her, from the tips of her fingers to the backs of her knees to the ends of her hair. He stood straight and tall, his dark hair in a wave across his forehead. She imagined him standing like this in front of an audience and wondered if his smile would be any less delightful if it were shared with dozens or hundreds of others.

She thought not.

"I would love to," he said, and drew the covering back from the piano's keys.

She watched him fold the drapery across the wide boards, taking great care with the cloth. As he sat on a small round stool, he met her eye. "I do hope my boasting hasn't raised your expectation for anything beyond the very basics of proficiency."

She smiled and perched on the edge of a covered sofa, folding her hands in her lap, and prepared to be only basically impressed.

From her seat, she watched his face as his fingers danced across the keys. She watched the muscles of his forearms move where they showed at the cuffs of his shirt.

It would be unfair for Hyacinth to accuse Mr. Harding of dishonesty, but his claim to be barely proficient was a far cry from the truth. He played well, his touch bringing out a depth and nuance that created emotions in Hyacinth that music rarely did. She had to consider that such feelings might not come solely from his song. He finished a piece and looked at her over the expanse of the large instrument.

She put a finger to her cheek as if in thought. "I have not yet decided how I feel about your performance. I believe I shall need another sample before I can know."

Lucas's tilted chin did not hide the smile blooming across his face at this suggestion of a compliment.

Between the music and the smile, she was certain this was a wonderful way to spend an evening.

Lucas played another song, and then another. Each song sent new thrills along Hyacinth's skin, and her heart seemed to beat in time with the music. She noticed that his choices felt similarly cheerful, even though the music was sophisticated. No broody Baroque numbers to add to the chill of the darkening manor. At last, he announced that she had heard everything he knew how to perform, and that tonight's concert had come to an end.

Hyacinth would have loved to beg for just one more piece, but she satisfied herself with the potential of another recital on another day. As he rose from the piano, she applauded his performance. "You are a man of many talents, Mr. Harding," she said.

He shook his head. "Only three."

"Three?" she asked. "Caretaking and piano performance I have seen. What is the third?"

His smile left her blushing. "I cannot be expected to unveil all my secrets at once, Miss Bell," he said simply.

He was teasing, and she was delighted by it. She had never felt so inclined to enjoy a man's flirting before. Tonight, she thought she'd rather have his attention than air to breathe.

She could most definitely practice patience until he decided it was time to show her another of his talents.

As the sun set, the wind rose, and the two heard groaning sounds coming through the stone walls as they made their way down the hall.

"Isn't that the loveliest, most melancholy noise?" Hyacinth asked, not really expecting agreement. He had made it clear he was not interested in ghost stories. But she could not pretend she wasn't delighted by the house's eerie accompaniment to their conversation.

"It's as if the walls were singing," Lucas replied.

Hyacinth drew closer to his arm, thinking his words were as lovely as a poem. "Exactly," she agreed. "Just like a dirge, a grieving song. I wonder what the house is mourning."

Lucas met her eyes. "Surely the absence of the master and his family."

Hyacinth made a humming sound. "Perhaps. But the flowers don't seem to be missing Mr. Whitbeck. They're thriving without his presence."

"They've been well taken care of by Mr. Gardner since the family left, I believe," Lucas said.

Hyacinth nodded. "Would you like to know a secret?"

Lucas gave her another of his spine-tingling smiles. "Always."

"Some orchids like to be left alone."

His brows arched in question. "As some people do?"

She nodded. "I imagine Mr. Whitbeck knows this and sent Mr. Gardner and his assistant so his flowers wouldn't get lonely. But I believe they would have done just fine on their own."

"But not for long," Lucas said. "Because of course, they need you."

"I'm sure the orchids thrived under the hand of Mr. Whitbeck's usual caretaker, but I am glad to be the replacement."

Leaning closer, Lucas whispered, "Would you like to know a secret?"

Hyacinth smiled, thrilled at how easily they had fallen into banter. "Always."

"I cannot regret the family's absence. If they were in residence, there would be no need for me here, and I would not have met you."

His sincerity took her breath away, and Hyacinth was unable to formulate an appropriate response. Instead of answering, she pressed his forearm with her fingers. She imagined the color in her cheeks told him the rest of what she could not articulate.

As their walk through the ground floor took them near the kitchen, Lucas nodded to a closed door. "Mrs. Carter's rooms are through there, in case you ever need her and she can't be found."

Hyacinth nodded, but knew only an extreme emergency would result in her knocking on that door. And even then, she would exhaust every other option first. The housekeeper had been so warm and friendly tonight, but it seemed only the presence of Mr. Harding brought out such kindness. Every other time she'd seen the woman, Hyacinth had been met with coldness, or at least stiffness. With Mrs. Carter's moods so changeable, Hyacinth would not intrude upon the woman if she could help it, and certainly not as a surprise.

The two made their way back to the entry hall, and Hyacinth led Lucas to the massive front doors. They stood there, backs against the doors, looking up at the twin curving staircases—one leading to her room and the other to a hall filled with darkness and mystery.

"I wonder," she mused, "what it would feel like to be welcomed into this house if it were full of people and lights and activity. How grand it must seem to climb those stairs outside, flanked by footmen, and enter to a view like this."

He nodded. "I can only truly imagine being one of the footmen, and even a position such as that might be beyond my reach. Household staff do not simply arrive and ask to be taught their responsibilities. Many of Mr. Whitbeck's household have trained all their lives to perform their duties to perfection."

"Is he a demanding man?" Hyacinth asked.

"For obvious reasons, our paths did not cross when I was a child," Lucas said. "But as master of the great house, he has a reputation for high expectations."

Hyacinth nodded. "I gathered as much. He seems rather proud of his home and his possessions. In one of his letters to me, he referred to his orchids as *treasures*," she said, giving the word particular emphasis. "He bade me safeguard the jewels of Ashthorne as though they were my own." She shook her head. "His love for his belongings might lead him to fancy tremendous stores of riches where there are simply strong walls, interesting paintings, and healthy flowers."

Lucas laughed. "Maybe you give him too much credit for his imagination. In fact, he may not be speaking in riddles. I grew up hearing tales of the treasures of Ashthorne. All of Suttonsbury village believes this place contains fortunes."

"Fortunes and ghosts," Hyacinth said, inspecting the shining brass doorknob behind them. "I suppose the villagers are not wrong," she said with a smile.

A clock chimed the hour, and Lucas pulled a watch from his waistcoat and made a sign of surprise.

"This is where I must leave you, Miss Bell," he said. "The hour has grown late, and I have neglected more than one of my duties this evening."

"I apologize that I stole your attention away from your caretaking." She smiled at him, not feeling sorry in the least.

He bowed his head over her fingers and brushed them

with the lightest touch of his lips. "I wish you a good night, then," he said, his voice soft and low.

"Good night," she repeated, and then thought, *Oh, and it is. Sweet dreams will surely attend me as I sleep.*

Hyacinth climbed the stairs, looking back once to see Lucas standing in the vestibule. He raised his hand in a wave, and she returned it with one of her own. Midway up the steps, she glanced toward the north staircase and the closed wing. She would not allow any unfulfilled wishes of spectral sightings to mar the sweetness of the day. Who needed the mystery of possible ghosts when men such as Lucas Harding existed?

Upon entering her room, she lit a taper, opened the window, and let in the sweet scent of night-blooming flowers and the songs of evening birds.

Hanging her gardening skirt in the unlocked wardrobe and placing her slightly dirtied blouse on the chair so she could brush it clean in the morning, she climbed into her nightdress and then into bed. Surrounded by sweet thoughts of Lucas Harding and both the delights and the delicious terrors of Ashthorne Hall, she drifted off to sleep.

LAMENT

Alone. Alone. Even the sound of the word is a cry.
Others live here, but I remain apart
To slip through time like driftwood on the water,
Making no ripple,
Leaving no impression.
Desolate.

CHAPTER 7

At the sound of moaning, Hyacinth sat up in bed, the half-closed window hangings dancing in the night's draft. Looking to the window, she stifled a scream. Something moved along the glass pane like a hand scrabbling for purchase.

She rubbed at her sleepy eyes. Surely, no one had climbed up the outer wall of Ashthorne Hall and attempted to enter through her window. Could a person even do that? She had to investigate. Swinging her legs out of bed, she felt the shock of her warm feet hitting the cold stone floor.

Moving toward the window, her steps were tiny and slow. She knew that whatever had startled her awake was simply a trick of the wind on stone, but now, standing in the darkness, surrounded by the sound of moans, the delightful fear she had felt touring the dim and shadowy hallways of Ashthorne with Lucas had lost its pleasurable coating. Hot waves of panic pulsed up her neck. Who could be reaching in her window? And how? The wind whipped her hair across her face, obscuring her vision even further, but she continued to place one foot before the other until she reached the window.

There is nothing to fear, she told herself. And then she told herself again. She placed her hands on the sill.

A black shape, darker than the night sky, pushed in and touched her hand.

Hyacinth shrieked and jumped back, her whole body flashing hot and then ice-cold in an instant. She felt a tingle across her scalp, as if each strand of her hair had grown a fraction of an inch simultaneously. Eyes wide and arms stretched out in front of her, she stared at the window, waiting for the ingress.

Within seconds, the shape pushed in again, and Hyacinth's hands flew to cover her mouth. Growing accustomed to the darkness surrounding her, she dared take her eyes off the window to scan the room for something useful with which to defend herself, for even if she let out a full-throated scream, who would hear her? Mrs. Carter's rooms were half a house away. Lucas Harding's cottage, even farther.

She spotted the yawning mouth of the empty fireplace along the wall opposite her bed. If she dared turn her back to the window, she might reach the fireplace poker before whomever—or whatever—was out there made entry, at which time she would have both feet solidly planted on stone floor while the intruder clung to the ivy growing up the walls of Ashthorne.

The ivy. Growing up the walls.

Ivy.

The thought turned over in her mind like a key hitting the tumblers of a lock. Armed not with a weapon but with a rational explanation, she felt the stiffness ease out of her spine from the top to the base as she saw the intruding shape for what it was: a branch of ivy blowing in the wind, its leaves like hands pushing into the room.

Berating herself for being a fool, her relief lasted only until the next gust of wind played against the stones of the manor, drawing out another deep and painful moan. Even with full understanding of the architectural cause of the sound, Hyacinth could not repress her shudder of dread. In concert with the arms of ivy, no one with a beating heart could fail to experience this trembling of fear, particularly in the middle of a dark night.

She stepped over to the fireplace, keeping an eye on the window. Wrapping her fingers around the handle of the poker somehow made her brave. Maybe it was a connection to the logical part of her mind, however scarcely it made itself known these days. Poker in hand, she walked with fractionally more confidence. She felt grateful that no one watched her tiptoe to the window, jab at the ivy leaves with the fireplace tool—just to be certain—and then close the window and draw the draperies tight.

If Hyacinth felt like a fool for climbing into bed with a hearthside poker in her hands, at least she gave herself credit for solving the mystery. And if an hour or more passed before she could relax enough to lie back against the pillows, no one ever had to know.

Even with the draperies covering the window, Hyacinth saw the line of cloudy light crossing her floor from the sunrise several hours later. Body aching from continued tension during the restless second half of the night, she maneuvered herself out of bed, still clutching the poker. She used the tool to lift the edge of her window drapes, allowing colorless light to pour into the room. She unwrapped her hand from the rod, feeling each finger prickle as the flow of blood returned.

Pushing the curtains all the way open, she stared out at the perfectly still autumn morning. The roof of an outbuilding peeked through a grove of trees, each leaf still painted a quiet and peaceful green. Soon the trees would put on their colorful cloaks, and then drop their leaves for winter.

Not a bird flew across her view. A low morning mist draped the fields in a gauzy sheet. Everything Hyacinth could see testified to the most lovely, peaceful sunrise. A simple, cloudy autumn morning. Exactly as it should be.

But a whisper of wind still echoed, just enough to shiver the ivy covering the outer walls. She had not dreamed it, she knew. But nothing of what she saw, felt, or heard now even hinted at the violence of her fear in the night.

Nothing but a single leaf of ivy, torn from its vine, its edges tattered from the beating it endured, resting on the floor beneath the window.

Hyacinth lifted the leaf, brought it close to her eyes, inspected it.

Only a leaf.

Not a threat.

She wanted to remember this logical answer to her midnight fear, so she carried the leaf to her bedside table. She would keep it there, as a talisman against further nighttime folly. As she laid the leaf upon the table, she saw a small pewter bowl half filled with strawberries.

A bowl she was certain had not been there when she lay down for bed the night before.

Upon arriving in the kitchen, Hyacinth expected to find the usual basket of bread and bowl of fruit. Instead, she saw Mrs. Carter and Lucas Harding, heads pressed close together in rapid, whispered conversation.

Mrs. Carter shook her head. "She must not know. She cannot. It won't be safe."

A new shudder ran across Hyacinth's shoulders like a tickle of intrigue. Stopping in the doorway, Hyacinth waited so as not to interrupt, and, whether she would admit it or not, wishing to hear more.

Lucas must have been looking for her. Without responding to Mrs. Carter's statements, he straightened and turned to Hyacinth with a smile of delight upon his face, a smile that felt to Hyacinth warm and sincere.

"Good morning," he said, stepping close to her and laying his hand gently upon her forearm, long fingers reaching toward her elbow.

Never had she imagined such a touch would feel so perfect. She smiled up at him in return.

"Good indeed," she said. "So calm. So quiet. So unlike last night."

Mrs. Carter darted a glance at Lucas and then at Hyacinth. "Did you have a restless night?" the housekeeper asked.

Hyacinth knew speaking the words would make her both

feel and sound like a fool, but she simply could not stay silent. "I thought I was being haunted," she said.

Mrs. Carter's hands flew to her open mouth, shock and terror clear in her eyes.

Lucas placed a hand on the housekeeper's arm, and Mrs. Carter stilled. Lucas sent another smile toward Hyacinth. "Whatever gave you that feeling?" he asked, his tone respectful of her former fears but appropriate to the light of the morning.

She turned to Mrs. Carter. "You know how this building weeps and moans. The breezes blew strong throughout the night."

"Like we heard it last night?" Lucas asked, reminding her—as if she needed reminding—of their walk together.

Hyacinth nodded. "Yes, but stronger. Louder."

"That does sound frightening," Lucas said. "And you felt as though something sinister was afoot?"

"Oh, no. The menacing part was the hand reaching into my room."

Mrs. Carter gave a yelp and looked at Lucas, her eyes wide. She turned back to Hyacinth. "You must bar your door. Every night. Without fail."

What did Mrs. Carter imagine Hyacinth had seen? An intruder inside the house? Silly. No one was here on the property but the three of them.

Unless Mrs. Carter knew about the ghost.

Unless she had seen it too. How exciting.

Hyacinth restrained a laugh so as not to offend the woman. "The hand did not come from the bedroom door. It reached in through the window. But as it happens, it was not a hand at all, but a vine of ivy blowing in through the open pane."

She saw Mrs. Carter relax a fraction.

"But fear not, I fought it off with a fireplace poker and my indomitable will." Hyacinth brought a fist to her hip in mimicry of the heroic poses she had seen in the portraits throughout the manor.

"Oh, dear," Mrs. Carter said, offering a shaky chuckle. "You had a dreadful fright."

Hyacinth did not wish the housekeeper to dwell on the misadventure, particularly if she was unwilling to offer any new information, so she gave another smile and assured her that the morning light had chased away any lingering fears. "The sunrise and the strawberries," she said. "Thank you for bringing them to me."

Shock passed over the housekeeper's features. "What strawberries?"

"The ones you brought to my room this morning. The ones in the pewter bowl. The ones left undamaged by the chicken."

Mrs. Carter stared at Hyacinth for too long before she forced a smile. "It was my pleasure. I'm happy to bring you anything that might make you more comfortable."

If the look Mrs. Carter and Lucas exchanged had been hidden from Hyacinth, the shake of his head was not. More secrets.

Mrs. Carter excused herself from the room, and Hyacinth pocketed a crusty bread roll and picked up a handful of cherries.

"May I escort you to the greenhouse?" Lucas asked, extending his arm.

On the path, Hyacinth felt Lucas's eyes on her, but he waited to speak until they were in the grove. "You spoke as though you were unafraid, but I worry you took your shock last night quite to heart."

Heart.

Lucas was giving her an opening to say more. To make a confession. To continue to strengthen the ties that were drawing them closer.

For a fraction of a moment, she wondered if she could tell him of the true condition of her heart. How quickly, how completely he had taken root in her soul and how she felt herself blooming. She would rather speak of tomorrow's future than of last night's fear. But she only met him yesterday. How silly would she sound if she confessed that she already admired him, possibly even adored him?

She looked at him, reading his earnestness along with a look of something more than polite concern. The speed with which she had found herself sincerely attached to him still took her by surprise, but she could see from his words and actions, he felt the same. She was not alone in her regard.

But there were secrets. Even after only one day.

She knew Lucas and Mrs. Carter had been speaking of her when she was not with them, because their conversation stopped when she entered the room. Despite the discomfort such knowledge added to her already muddled feelings, she was delighted and surprised by their obvious mutual attraction, an unanticipated addition to her employment in Mr. Whitbeck's garden.

All of these thoughts danced through her mind before she responded to his solicitation.

"I felt deeply afraid. And then deeply silly," she told him honestly. She glanced up at him. "Do you think I really ought to bar my door as Mrs. Carter said? If she and I are the only ones in the house, what danger could possibly befall me?"

"There is nothing in the manor that will hurt you," Lucas answered.

Hyacinth doubted that was true. But her mind was full of far more than decorative hanging swords and rooms crammed full of unused furnishings. She thought of her privacy.

According to Mrs. Carter, last evening's strawberries had been destroyed by a rogue chicken in the kitchen. Yet they had appeared—or at least most of them—whole and unblemished in a bowl left on her nightstand by someone she had neither seen nor heard, sometime between her falling asleep and waking.

The ivy blunder had her questioning what she'd seen, what she thought she understood. But notwithstanding her misunderstanding about the intrusion through the window, someone *had* come into her bedroom in the night.

And yet she could not say the words to Lucas. Why was that? Fear, certainly. Fear that it had been him, sneaking into the manor, up the stairs, down the vast hallway, and into her room. Fear that it had been him, breaking all manner of rules of propriety, decency. Fear that it had been him, behaving unacceptably.

If it had been Lucas, she had misjudged his character deeply.

But if it had not been Lucas, someone else had stolen into her room in the dark of night.

Someone else. But who?

She said nothing. There was nothing she could say that would not make this awkward situation more uncomfortable. She could continue to collect data. She could wait.

With no further questions or confessions from either of them, Lucas left her at the door to the orchid house and went about his work.

Hyacinth worked until the sun rose to the center of the sky, then she set aside her tools and her notes. She walked to the table where Eleanor sat, her leaves and remaining blossoms looking strong and well.

"Eleanor, you are so brave. Even after a tumble, look how you're holding on."

She lifted the new pot in which her prized orchid grew and examined the underside of her leaves. "I think this hothouse is good for you, but I miss you when you're not in the room with me. Perhaps I shall bring you inside the big house to sleep, at least some of the time. I should hope to be as bold and resilient as you are. But I have far to go, you know. There's a whole manor house that is off-limits to me, and I have barely even set foot in the forbidden sections. That's not very like me, is it?"

She set Eleanor's pot carefully back on the table next to trays of rooting compound. She leaned close and whispered to the orchid, "I believe it's time for me to see what I can see."

Mrs. Carter had left no doubt about her rules, but Hyacinth Bell was not one to obey without question, especially when there was evidence to gather. The housekeeper could not be everywhere at once, after all. No one could.

Hyacinth walked toward the kitchen door, unsure if she'd rather find Mrs. Carter or not. If she saw the housekeeper, she would know where the woman was working and could explore without any need for explanation, but if she did not see her, she could not know where Mrs. Carter was working.

Mrs. Carter was not in the kitchen, and as Hyacinth moved past some of the sitting rooms, she stopped and listened. She heard sounds of cleaning: small objects being moved, a quiet humming, cloth whisking across furniture.

Perfect.

With quiet steps, Hyacinth walked to the foot of her staircase. If she was caught in defiance of Mrs. Carter's rules, she could claim she was on her way to her bedroom. Even with this plan in her mind, she could not help but look up the north staircase to the forbidden hallway. The position of the autumn afternoon sun seemed to cast more shadows on that hallway than on her own.

At the top of the stairs, Hyacinth put her hand to the knob of the first door. It was locked tight, as she expected. She could move down the hall and try each door; surely Mrs. Carter had missed locking one or two. She turned toward the next room, but instead, she stiffened her spine and reminded herself that she was a person not so easily defeated.

Ashthorne Hall was hiding something, and Hyacinth would discover what it was.

Undeterred by a simple bedroom door, she leaned down and inspected the locking mechanism, sure that, with the help of a pair of hairpins, she could enter, just as she had done to her older sister's room in years long past.

She grasped the handle and rattled the knob, feeling the solid wood construction and the snug fit of the door in its casing.

"Very solid workmanship. Well done, builders," she murmured. She knelt, holding her eye to the knob. The metal surrounding the lock was scratched and scuffed, scraped as if by picks or pins.

"Ah. I am not the only one who considers a locked door a worthy challenge." She wondered if one of the Whitbeck children shared her tendency to enter rooms forbidden to them. The thought made her chuckle and then firm her resolve.

Pulling out two pins from her hair, she made a few cursory stabs at the lock, her movements made more awkward than usual by the heavy shadows in the hall and her nerves fluttering at the possibility of discovery.

Shaking her head, she pushed all thoughts of Mrs. Carter into the back of her mind and renewed her efforts.

When she could feel the resistance of tumblers within the lock, she wiggled and twisted until the lock sprang free.

"Ha," she said, then held her hand to her mouth. Instead of crowing in pleasure, she patted the doorknob and smiled to herself.

Hyacinth stood upright and stepped into the room. The first thing she noticed was the movement of the holland covers over the furnishings. The second was the strength of the breeze. She moved to the wall and put her hands to the open window, wondering why Mrs. Carter would leave a window thrown wide in a locked room.

A careful exploration of the room would take longer than the few minutes she had, but she made her way along the walls, passing each item of furniture, running her hand over desk and dresser, armoire and bedposts. She lifted covers on each painting and mirror. What, she wondered, did she think she might find? A chest of treasure? A pirate's map? A warren for the spirits that haunted the manor?

Nothing startling appeared in her search. In fact, the room felt quite familiar. Even with the dustcloths shrouding the furnishings, Hyacinth could see how its appointments compared to her own. A dressing table. A stand beside the bed. Another black cabinet, locked, just like the one in her bedroom.

A clock chimed somewhere in the manor, and she made her way back to the door, careful to ease her way out slowly in case Mrs. Carter had finished cleaning the sitting room and moved toward the stairs.

Hyacinth hurried down the hall to her own room, heart thrumming with excitement as she ran along the carpeted floor. She had done it. Entered a forbidden room. With this success behind her, what adventure was outside her reach? Now that she had made her way into a locked room, what would stop her from trying a door or two in the forbidden hallway? She felt great delight in the prospect of continued exploration. She grinned, knowing she could enter the manor's locked rooms any time the fancy struck her, and the very idea made her feel more than ever at home.

LAMENT

Though no door is barred to me, I am no less restricted than a prisoner.

I must be always alone, with memories of illness and death lingering

Stronger than any thoughts of long-ago joy.

What happiness have I felt here? Only that of secrecy,

Of giving small gifts.

And of knowing someone remembers the woman I used to be.

I must not let them forget.

CHAPTER 8

Hyacinth reveled in the vast expanse of Mr. Whitbeck's garden structures. In addition to the orchid house, which—like the other hothouses—held a stove and a giant tub of water so the building was warm and humid all year, there were several greenhouses, some near the orchid house and others farther afield, each paneled in glass and protected from the elements, but unheated. The warmth in those buildings was provided by the sun and the plants growing within.

When the family was in residence at the manor house, Hyacinth could imagine the full complement of gardeners for both the grounds and the indoor structures, tending flowers for cut arrangements as well as some of the more tender fruit trees. Now the greenhouses, dripping with near-constant rain, were mostly left fallow, growing trays of ground cover, mosses, and flowering shrubs in pots, perhaps anticipating a return to the inside of the manor.

There was a glorious solarium, its greened-copper frame blending in with the trees and shrubberies, set in a lovely garden walled in on three sides. Along one of the lines of hedges, a plot of wildflowers ran in a riot of blues and purples. Hyacinth found the view so picturesque she sat on a stone bench tucked under a sprawling tree with her feet in the damp grass and made a sketch of the hedge, eager to add in a touch of color so she could keep the memory of it with her always.

A small and unreasonable wish developed in a secret part of her heart to hold a wedding right there in the solarium, with the afternoon light streaming through the leaves.

On her way back to the orchid hothouse, Hyacinth passed the formal rose garden complete with stone fountain. Some of the bushes had late-blooming roses still showing off their petals. Someone, possibly Mr. Gardner, had taken care to lop off the dead rose hips after their first bloom so they could blossom again. She wished she could have seen the whole garden on its best day, when the family was in residence, fountain running with a bubbling stream of clear water. Perhaps guests dancing by candlelight. Not at any specific event, of course. Not necessarily at a marriage celebration. Simply a party. Of course.

Hyacinth laughed at herself. Did every beautiful element of the estate exist merely to become a backdrop to her fantasy wedding? She knew she was being silly, but the silliness amused her, and no one else would ever know.

At midday, Mrs. Carter put her head into the orchid house and called for Hyacinth. "Miss Bell?" Almost immediately she called again, this time with more force. "Miss Bell."

Each interaction with the housekeeper reinforced Hyacinth's understanding that she was not a patient woman.

Rather than shout across the tables, she hurried over to the door, rubbing dirt from her hands.

"I am on my way into the village. Is there anything you need?" Mrs. Carter asked. A polite question, but asked without any warmth.

"How very kind," Hyacinth said. She could at least pretend it was so. "I believe Mr. Gardner has something for me, but I had planned to walk into town after I've finished here. Perhaps I will cross your path there?"

Mrs. Carter made a scoffing sound. "I wouldn't assume that any of the things I need to keep the manor alive would be found in George Gardner's little shop. No. I have other destinations."

Something in her words tickled Hyacinth's mind, a thought she couldn't quite grasp. She wanted Mrs. Carter to keep talking.

"You've been there?" Hyacinth asked.

Mrs. Carter nodded. "Gardner's been a fixture in Suttonsbury as long as I can remember. A decent grower and a friendly neighbor, but he's lost his mind bringing on that man as an assistant."

Ah, Hyacinth thought. *The secret opinions of the stoic Mrs. Carter might be uncovered here in the hothouse.* She wanted to keep the housekeeper invested in the discussion, even if it bordered on gossip. "Do you mean James? The man who came to help with the orchids?"

With a shake of her head, Mrs. Carter said, "He was no help at all, wandering across the estate as if he had any right to explore it." She glanced at Hyacinth before adding, "I told him to clear off the place and asked George not to bring him back. Lucky you arrived when you did." She brushed her hands together as if making a physical break from the conversation.

Hyacinth wondered if she made herself too much at home if Mrs. Carter would tell her to clear off as well.

She'd have to be much more subtle in her investigations than James had been.

Mrs. Carter said, "Nothing from the village, then?" as though Hyacinth had answered her original question, then turned from the doorway and walked away.

Hyacinth agreed with Mrs. Carter's obvious distaste for Mr. Gardner's assistant, but she wished she could know more about the housekeeper's reasons. Was she concerned by his rude demeanor? By his distasteful insolence? There were a variety of explanations why a person would be turned off by the man James.

But then another thought pushed that one aside—Mrs. Carter's phrase "Keep the manor alive."

This was how she described her work.

The phrase suggested that, without her superintendence, the manor might die.

Mrs. Carter spoke of the great stone house as though it breathed. Of course, when Hyacinth thought about it, considering how much wind moved down the hallways at night, it was probably the most precise way of describing it. And it had not truly occurred to Hyacinth until now how much was expected of Mrs. Carter. What a heavy responsibility. Not only the daily management of the near-empty house but also keeping it at readiness for such time as any of the family would come back. Simply to put aside the cloths draped over every piece of furniture would take days.

She could not fully imagine the momentous tasks at hand for a housekeeper at an estate like Ashthorne. It was no wonder Mrs. Carter did not seem to have much time to be friendly with her. The woman had far more to do than Hyacinth could even imagine. Naturally she could not be bothered to amuse an unexpected houseguest, even if the guest entertained premature hopes of someday becoming a family member.

Hyacinth shook that thought off and returned to her work, but only minutes passed before she realized she was missing her best opportunity to investigate the house.

Mrs. Carter was away in the village. The manor was empty.

Giddy with the chance before her, Hyacinth hurried back to the house. Through the trees, she caught a glimpse of Mrs. Carter walking along the winding lane leading to the road, a large basket on her arm. Without a cart or carriage, the housekeeper could not stop at many shops. If the road into Suttonsbury was about a mile—and Hyacinth thought it was longer—and Mrs. Carter walked swiftly, she might make the round trip in forty minutes. She had suggested there was more than one stop she needed to make in town. Hyacinth made a quick calculation and decided she had at least an hour.

Perfect.

She began her exploration in the kitchen, where several doors stood along the back wall. Hyacinth opened three of them in turn. Behind the first, she discovered a cupboard holding a neat and orderly supply of brooms, mops, cloths, and buckets. On her most industrious day, she couldn't imagine the uses for so many cleaning supplies. One more measure of Mrs. Carter's diligence.

The second door opened onto a short, descending staircase. From the light from the kitchen, Hyacinth could make out several stairs and a landing, and then the steps turned. The cool air suggested a food storage room, and the smell of dirt hinted at potatoes. Another day, she would happily explore this passage, but she'd not waste her hour alone in the manor looking at bins of vegetables.

The next door, the one closest to the outer wall of the room, was the most promising. Another staircase, but this one led both up and down. Unlike the house's main stairways, there was no plush carpet, and only a metal ring for a lamp sconce. This was not a staircase for the family. This was for the help.

The servants' stairway. Her father's house had one. Most large houses did, so the staff would not be seen. It also made an excellent hiding place for a young girl intent on disappearing from her older sister's critical eye.

Hyacinth lit a small oil lamp from the kitchen counter and slipped into the staircase.

The same chill wind that moved in her bedroom's hallway blew through this narrow staircase. She climbed and then leveled, climbed and then leveled, counting at least two dozen steps when she realized the strange pattern suggested the staircase hugged the outer wall of the manor while avoiding the windows. Clearly this passage ran between the bedrooms and the building's outer walls. Soon the steps flattened out into a landing and a hallway, and by holding her lamp high, she could see it ran long and straight enough to be the upstairs hall at the end of which lay her own room. When she came to a door, she turned the knob. She pushed and then pulled the door, but it would not give. She pulled out a hairpin and, with the confidence of previous success, set to unlocking the bedroom door.

This lock was different. Perhaps a newer addition to the manor, its mechanism did not open as easily as the door she'd tried yesterday. A second pin did not help. She fussed with the pins, but the tumblers would not pop the lock open for her.

The lamplight illuminated a small plate on the door with a number on it. A label for the room. From this back hallway, servants could be sure to approach the correct rooms. Hyacinth felt a thrill knowing she could open any of these rooms from the main hall, even if it would be far more convenient to do so from this hidden passageway.

She left the first door and moved to the next. Also numbered. Also locked tight.

She would figure out a way to get through these doors, but her search might require a different device.

Hyacinth would need to find a key—or something to act as a key. She reached into her pocket where she kept some of her smallest garden tools close at hand. Her shears were far too big to be of any use on these locks, and the blade of her cutting knife bent too easily.

The tools were critical to her work in the hothouse, but useless in this endeavor.

Because she was not a person who let her luck go untested, Hyacinth tried all the remaining doors in the hallway; each proved inaccessible. Only when she approached the end of the hall and turned the knob that she was sure must provide entry to her own room did she find one unlocked. Not only unlocked. Unlatched.

A frisson of fear ran down her spine. At the end of this long, deserted hallway, only the entry to her room was open.

Who might be using this staircase, moving through the manor invisibly?

It must be Mrs. Carter, Hyacinth told herself. It had to be.

But why would she need to use the hidden stairs? No one was in residence who cared if Mrs. Carter was visible in her work.

Hyacinth had seen the housekeeper moving with confidence through the main hallways; it was even the way she had shown Hyacinth to her quarters.

Why, then, was *this* door unlocked?

Hyacinth pushed open the door, only then realizing she had never noticed the other side of this door from inside her bedroom. She would have seen a door in the wall, even if she'd been distracted by so many unexpected things since her arrival.

She stepped through and was met by another door, also locked up tight. Again, the pin was useless. She rapped the door with her knuckles. Solid. A connecting door?

She made a mental map of her bedroom, placing bed and armoire, tables and fireplace.

This door must be the black painted cabinet beside the window.

The one she had been unable to open from inside her room.

Frustrated that she was mere feet from her own bed but unable to enter the room, she kicked at the door.

A sound she did not expect met her. A rustle and a kick in return. Could the arrangement of the servants' staircase create an echo? Did she imagine it?

But then Hyacinth heard a scuffle and another thud against the door. A deep growl. A man's voice, muttering. This voice, so different from Lucas's gentle speech, grated against her ears and her nerves. Deep, angry, unfamiliar snarls.

No. This was not her imagination. Someone was in her bedroom. Someone had heard her from behind the wall and wanted her to know he was there.

Her room was not her own. Another person was inside it. It was not Mrs. Carter nor was it Lucas, and, Hyacinth feared, the stranger was not there to leave a gift of berries or flowers.

Without another thought, she turned and ran, holding the lamp in front of her and passing locked door after locked door and then down, never stopping until she reached the landing that led to the kitchen. Surrounded by the doors leading to the cleaning closet and the storage cellar, she knew she would soon relax enough to catch her breath. Heart pounding from exertion as well as shock, she turned the knob to reenter the warm, bright room, but the door would not open.

No. Locked? How?

A cry of frustration escaped her lips, and she rattled the knob and pushed against it with her shoulder.

No good. It didn't give even a bit.

Hyacinth spun around in her fright and looked at the other doors at this landing, and she saw a different one had a line of daylight streaming beneath it.

Reaching for that door, she turned the knob and was immediately relieved to be in the kitchen. She had, in her confusion and fear, tried to get out of the servants' hallway through the wrong door.

A few shaky breaths helped calm her. A silly mistake, but one she thought now she would not repeat. Next time she explored the hidden staircase, she would recognize which door led back to the warmth of the kitchen.

Now that she was safe in the familiar room, she chided herself for her foolishness. Surely no one was in her bedroom. She had imagined the knocking and the gravelly voice muttering from the other side of the door. The house was empty. The halls were silent, as always. They must be.

Her overactive imagination had caused her to become turned around. The locked door behind the kitchen wall— the one she tried by mistake but could not open—must lead to the north wing.

A flurry of anticipation filled Hyacinth as she imagined making her way along this hidden hallway, a new way to explore the rooms closed to her. A secret passage through the forbidden spaces of Ashthorne.

But first, she would need to find the key that unlocked the doors in the servants' hallway.

Her breathing back to its normal rate, Hyacinth turned to the kitchen's storage cupboards and pulled open several drawers, but she was unsurprised to find nothing useful in her search. Surely Mrs. Carter kept the house keys with her at all times.

She did find a cache of candles and matches, and she liberated a few of each to take back up to her room.

Once upstairs, she opened her door slowly, almost sure she would find the room empty. Only a tiny corner of her brain wished for proof of what she'd heard from the other side of the wall, the fright she'd experienced still heavy on her mind. Nothing unusual except for a strange but familiar lingering smell. Tobacco? Did she imagine that scent? Surely no one had been smoking a pipe in her bedroom. Maybe it was simply a whiff of fireplace ash.

No. She'd heard the scuffle. She'd heard the voice. Someone had been here.

With a shake of her head, she placed the candles and matches on her bedside table, easily within reach if a late-night exploration opportunity arose. Candles would be perfect for such expeditions. A lamp would better protect a flame from the breezes in the hallways, but a lamp was difficult to hide if she was discovered, while a candle could be pinched out and placed in a pocket.

Hyacinth laughed at herself. What had a few days at Ashthorne Hall done to her? Was she now a person who snuck around in the dark, planning ways to hide her steps from the prying eyes of the housekeeper?

As she settled the matches and candles on the table so they would not fall, she saw something small and round. A perfect, tiny shell, tinged blue and white. Had this shell come from the shoreline? Would Mrs. Carter have left this for her?

It seemed such a strange thing for the housekeeper to do, so out of her usual character, but Hyacinth couldn't imagine how else it might have arrived on her bedside table.

She turned to study the large black cabinet against the wall. In the afternoon light, it was far less an object of mystery, and she was certain that if she could open the door, it would lead her into the servants' staircase.

She pulled a few pins from the neat pile on her dressing table and knelt again in an attempt to unfasten the door.

When she looked at the locking mechanism this time, she noticed the same appearance of nicks and scratches she'd seen in that first door in the hallway. Had that only been yesterday?

Perhaps the person who had tried that lock had not been one of the Whitbeck children at all. Could it have been the man who had entered her room? Could he be searching Ashthorne Hall as well?

The thought, though disquieting, made her more eager than ever to find a way through this door.

Several minutes and a few finger pricks later, Hyacinth was still no closer to unlocking the door. Where would Mrs. Carter store extra keys? For surely there were several sets; maids and cleaners would need to move through the hidden staircases to go about their work. If the house were full of family and staff, Hyacinth could borrow a key from any of the maids. There must be a cache of keys somewhere in the manor. Might she attempt a search of Mrs. Carter's room?

No. That was a step too far. The housekeeper could make free to enter Hyacinth's room, because she had work that brought her there. Even if the idea of her entry made Hyacinth uncomfortable, there were excuses for Mrs. Carter to be in her bedroom, but not for Hyacinth to take such a liberty with the housekeeper's private quarters. Besides, she feared the time drew near for Mrs. Carter's return from the village.

Best she set aside her explorations for now and make her way into Suttonsbury to gather the last of the supplies for the orchids.

Hyacinth knew only one way into the village, and she

kept her eyes open for Mrs. Carter. She did not see the lady on the path and assumed Mrs. Carter had at least a few more stops to make as she took care of her errands. The walk into the village was uneventful, and Hyacinth enjoyed the break from the rain as a hint of sun shone through patchy afternoon clouds, which scudded along toward the village as if pushed by the waves at the shore.

As she neared Suttonsbury, small cottages appeared along the road, then slightly larger dwellings. Crooked rooflines suggested not only the houses' age but also the likelihood that they'd been reconstructed now and then, adding rooms as families grew. If the asymmetrical dwellings were any indication, many families must have rebuilt their homes over the years.

Hyacinth hadn't previously considered the inconveniences of the lives of the villagers any more than she'd ever thought about the families in the villages surrounding her father's house in the country, and she wondered now at her thoughtlessness. How simple for her, living in a huge house with more rooms than one could ever need, to ignore the realities of those whose lives were so different from her own.

Before long, the road turned, and Mr. Gardner's shop sign came into view. A shiver of discomfort ran through her as she imagined meeting Mr. Gardner's assistant James again. She had no wish to speak with him, or for him to talk to her.

Luck was on her side, though, for she saw Mr. Gardner as soon as she opened the door. She entered the shop and found the kindly little man standing behind the counter, handing a large parcel to a woman wrapped in a snug shawl.

"This should increase your yield. Mix half into the soil at the end of harvest and let it lie over the winter. Then at planting time, add the rest, making sure to mix it well. This is powerful, and it can burn your plants if you overuse it."

The woman thanked him, and Hyacinth held the door open for her as she left the shop.

"Ah, Miss Bell. How nice to see you again," Mr. Gardner said, his cheeks as pink as peony petals. "So glad you could come pick up your parcel." He looked over his shoulder as if to ensure they were alone. "James offered to deliver it, but I was counting on sharing a cup of tea with you."

Hyacinth recalled the sneering, threatening way James had spoken to her the night of her arrival and was glad she'd insisted on coming here. She did not fancy running into James at Ashthorne, especially after the frights she'd experienced recently.

"I don't mind the walk in the least," she said, hoping Mr. Gardner would offer more information about his employee, but not daring to invite gossip outright.

He did not disappoint her.

"James seems a difficult sort, rather sour and gruff, and he doesn't know much about gardening, but he's strong enough to lift and move the things I can't. His help, for what it's worth, is appreciated for as long as it may last."

Hyacinth could tell by the way the man couched a negative comment within a compliment that he knew a thing or two about gossiping. Mr. Gardner would be a pleasant ally in the village.

She remembered what Mrs. Carter had told her about the onset of James's employment. "Has he not been here long?" she asked.

Mr. Gardner shook his head and led her to a small table

in the corner where a pot of tea sat ready for them. He poured her a cup. "He arrived very recently. Only a few months ago, just after the family left the big house. I brought him up to the manor to help with the flowers, but I believe he might be better suited to running the shop in my absence."

Hyacinth nodded, even though she doubted the surly man made a positive impression on Mr. Gardner's customers.

She smiled at Mr. Gardner as she sipped her tea. "I appreciate the good care you took of the orchids between Mr. Whitbeck's departure and my arrival. You are kind to take on more work, and I hope it didn't cause trouble for you."

Mr. Gardner's laugh shook his round stomach. He set his cup in its saucer and ran his fingers along the length of his beard. "If anyone caused me trouble, it was not Mr. Whitbeck. And certainly not yourself. My man James doesn't need any help from you or me or anyone to find trouble. As soon as I can find another young person willing to help me in the shop and the greenhouse, I expect I'll turn him out. He's had warnings, but still, he wanders away, leaving the shop for hours at a time, and rarely has his mind fully on any job I've given him."

Hyacinth felt alarmed that Mr. Gardner had to trust his business to such an unsavory employee. The shock must have shown on her face because Mr. Gardner shook his head and smiled at her.

"This is a rather unpleasant discussion, I fear," Mr. Gardner said. "If you've finished your tea, let's find you those stakes Mr. Whitbeck ordered."

As Hyacinth followed Mr. Gardner out the back door of the shop and into the greenhouse, she asked about the fertilizer the woman had purchased. "Would it be helpful to the orchids, do you think?"

"Ah, I wondered the same thing. If you're willing to make a bit of an experiment, I'll order a package of it for you. I could have it here in a few days."

"I'd love to give it a try. Thank you."

They walked through the greenhouse to where Mr. Gardner had gathered the small boxes of plant stakes that were the last of Mr. Whitbeck's order.

"You just let me know what else you might want. There's a whole section in our ledgers for Mr. Whitbeck's purchases, and you may charge anything you need to his account."

"Thank you very much," Hyacinth said. "I appreciate your kindness."

He patted her arm and smiled up at her. "It's a pleasure to work with you, even from a distance."

"Well, if it's any use to you, you're always welcome to come to the manor for a visit. At least to the orchid house. We could share a cup of tea with the caretaker, perhaps."

The thought of sitting for a visit with both Mr. Gardner and Lucas almost made her laugh with anticipation. How delightful it would be to have these two kindhearted and gentle men in the same room together.

His smile matched hers, and she hoped the sweet man would take her invitation to heart. She was always grateful for another friendly face.

LAMENT

I have cried over my loneliness, but I fear it's better than the alternative.

Someone else has taken to wandering these silent halls.

Someone who moves in secret but leaves a lingering feeling of malice.

Even through my ruined nose, I can smell the rank odors of stale smoke and drink, unwashed clothing and filth.

I fear he looks for me.

He would ask something of me.

Even if I was inclined to show myself to him,

I doubt I could give him what he wants.

I cannot remember the simple ways of human interaction.

Far too much has changed.

CHAPTER 9

The next day in the orchid house, Hyacinth kept her rubber bulb mister in her pocket, giving each plant a whisper of water and a compliment, encouraging them in their good work of profligate expansion.

Upon exploring the last of the air roots, Hyacinth peeled the gloves from her hands, chattering to the orchid she'd named Gladys, a Dendrobium with deep purple petals and a record number of swelling buds.

"Gladys," Hyacinth said, "your blossoms are about to astonish all who see you." She gave Gladys's pot a quarter turn. "Today promises rain, and lucky for you, for you love the rain, don't you? So much moisture in the air. Orchids love the rain as long as it does not come through the windows."

Her voice took on a singsong lilt as she misted and turned and inspected the lower leaves, a melody forming from the silliness of the moment. "As long as it does not come through the windows. As long as it stays outside where it belongs, and you continue to enjoy a perfect balance of humidity and breeze for optimal growth and reduced chance of rot."

A voice from behind joined Hyacinth's. "I am quite sure that I love the rain," Lucas said, speaking in a rhythmic lilt himself, "but I shall never love a storm as much as I adore"— he paused for a beat as he gently turned her to face him and looked deeply into her eyes, and then he continued—"this song."

Hyacinth laughed, partly from her own silliness and partly from his jest, which left her cheeks reddening. No hint of shame stirred her. She warmed from his presence. She watched him as he gazed at her face, that soft smile lighting his handsome features. She wished he could stay in the hothouse all day. Every day. With her.

Only days ago, such a statement from him would have rendered her speechless, but now she found she was quite capable of making a joke in return.

"I am very grateful for your compliment, sir," Hyacinth said with a bow. "Was it the clever subtleties of the lyrics that caught your attention? Or my exceptional performing voice?" She was under no delusions about her singing. She was capable of carrying a tune, but no more. Her voice might be described as pleasant, if the person doing the describing was already fond of her.

"I believe there are far too few songs that make use of the word *rot*, in fact," he said. "It packs a great deal of power into a very small syllable, not to mention its visual imagery."

"And there are so many useful rhymes, if rhyming songs are your preference," Hyacinth added. "Words like *trot* and *forgot*."

He nodded, giving her a serious look as though this might be a truly important discussion. "Blot. Fought. Caught." He laughed and then stopped, his face growing serious. "Oh, speaking of caught. Will you please tell me if you see anyone in or near the manor house? I saw a man walking along the clifftop who ought not to have been there."

Before she could comment on his accidental use of "ought not," her feelings of delight at their playful conversation flew away as quickly as a leaf on the wind. "In or near the manor house? Do you mean *inside* the house?"

She thought of the person muttering and knocking in her bedroom while she stood on the other side of the locked door. She supposed her nervousness was written all over her face. She had not imagined any of it, as much as she'd tried to convince herself she was being dramatic.

Could a stranger simply walk into Ashthorne Hall? Without a full house staff to monitor the huge building, it seemed conceivable. A man walking along the cliff simply strolls into the manor. It wasn't a leap in logic to assume he was the person making sounds in her room.

Was that the reason Mrs. Carter had warned her to bar her door at night?

Lucas glanced at her face and shook his head. "Oh, dear. I should not have said that. I meant within the property. Please don't be afraid." His face fell.

His response shook her out of her gloom. She gave a rueful chuckle. "You may not give me a shock like that and then demand I feel no fear. I believe such a command can only be ignored."

Lucas lowered his brows, and she wondered if she had offended him. "Please accept my apology. I should never have mentioned it. I only wanted to keep you aware so you remain in perfect safety." He leaned closer to her and lowered his voice. "In my imagination, I often gravitate toward the worst possible outcome. Hyacinth, I am sorry I let myself assume the worst and caused you to do the same."

She only halfway heard his apology, her mind catching on the sound of her name on his lips. She felt she was floating, even as her nerves jangled from his news.

How could one person feel so many things all at once? A body could only take so much. She thought she might need to sit down.

With another look at Lucas, at his concern and attentiveness, she felt herself grow more relaxed. What a tremendous power, the ability to bestow calm. He had a talent to change her feelings rapidly, that was certain. Quite a remarkable man, this Lucas Harding. If he could work such magic, she could at least pretend not to be scared.

Hyacinth nodded. "I will be aware but unafraid. If you think such a thing is possible, I will do it."

"I'm afraid I ruined our game," he said, his voice still gloomy.

She shook her head. "Of course not. We are poets. A little shock to our systems is exactly what will summon the muse. Don't you know this is how all the best poets find inspiration?"

"Inspiration to find more rhyming words for rot?" he said, his smile proving how pleased he was at the return to their playfulness.

"Distraught. Fraught." She raised her eyebrows at that one, as if it came as a surprise to her.

He played along at once, looking grateful. "Indeed. Well done. Sought. Plot. Dot. Yacht."

"We are very good at this. Perhaps," she said, "we ought to write a song together."

He laughed, delighted. "What a wonderful idea. What shall we sing about?"

"I believe I have covered the benefits of keeping orchids out of the rain," she said. "So that leaves us the three best ways to prepare a potato and the benefits of visiting the seaside at Brighton."

"Well, I have vast experience with both of these topics," he said. "So I shall be helpful."

Hyacinth removed her gloves and brushed the front of her apron, removing most of the debris from the day's work. "The best songs are written sitting down."

"Truly?"

"Surely everyone knows this." She led him to the chairs and pulled out her notebook. With a flourish of her pencil, she declared herself ready to declaim. "We need only agree on a topic," she said.

He removed his jacket and folded it over the back of his chair. Hyacinth chose to concentrate on the pleasure of his comfort rather than the surprise of his casual removal of his outerwear. She reminded herself that city manners did not translate to country living.

"All the best songs are love songs," Lucas said. "So perhaps we ought to attempt to write that." He folded his arms across his chest, his sleeves pulling up and giving her a welcome view of his muscled forearms.

Hyacinth laughed to cover another blush. "I know more about potatoes."

"Very well, we can write a love song to potatoes."

How was it so easy for him to move between moods? Was it only a minute ago he was apologizing for his sullenness?

She wanted to help him stay in his cheerful, playful state. "That is a very specific genre," she said.

Lucas nodded, his face all seriousness. "And do you think there is anyone who would not be able to relate to it?"

Hyacinth laughed again. She adored these stolen moments with Lucas, and was thrilled to discover that none of the fear brought about by his mentioning the stranger now remained in her heart. "We may just create the universal ballad. How shall we begin?"

Lucas put his hand to his chin in an attitude of deep consideration. "I believe the typical practice of songwriters is to make a list of all the ways in which the object embodies perfection. This should be easy with potatoes. They are warm, and soft, and tender."

So was his glance at her. She felt herself warming in response.

He smiled at her. "Are you writing this down?"

Of course. She had a job to do. Hyacinth scratched the words onto her paper.

Lucas nodded. "Good. What else? Comforting. And comfortable. Even when they have been prepared in a new way, there is something familiar. That feeling we all desire to come back to."

Hyacinth scribbled his words as fast as she could. "I

rather like their shape," she mused. "One could almost mistake them for a stone."

"Oh, yes indeed," Lucas said. "I believe the hallmark of a truly relatable love song is comparing the beloved to rocks. How else could we work in words like *lumpen* and *boulder* after all?"

Hyacinth looked down at the words she had written on the page. "I believe we may have aimed too high attempting to write the ode to a potato on our first try. Perhaps we would do better to write about ordinary humans and try our hands at the often-traveled flower metaphors."

He nodded. "Bloom of youth. Lips like petals and the like."

"Exactly," she said.

Lucas smiled at her, and she was surprised to find how familiar his smile had become. After only days at Ashthorne together, he was known to her, and she to him.

He said, "I have always liked flower images, but I confess, I am not convinced anyone has a mouth that looks like a daisy. Or an iris."

The image made her laugh again. "Indeed, if I saw someone with a mouth resembling a larkspur, I should deliver them to a doctor at once. But I've always believed the comparison was less in what they look like and more in their feel to the touch."

"That's silly. People don't have skin that feels like flowers."

She looked surprised. "I do," she said, touching her finger to her lower lip.

"Your lips feel like petals?" he asked, squeezing his hands together as if attempting to keep them still.

She hoped it meant he wanted to reach over and touch her mouth as much as she wanted him to. The thought shocked her, but in a delicious way. She had never felt so attracted to anyone.

She forced herself to swallow, and she looked at the table in front of her. It was very difficult to hold his gaze under such conditions. She was not willing to leave such an opening unattended, however. She glanced back up at Lucas.

"I have spent quite some time with flowers," she said with a measure of calm she did not feel. "In my training, you understand. Possibly more time than most people. In addition, I have had this mouth all my life. I feel it is safe to say that I am the expert here."

"You mean," he said, pointing to the nearest table of flowers, "if I were to touch this orchid, for instance, and your mouth, I should find them indistinguishable?"

She looked shocked. "Oh, heavens, no. You cannot touch them. Under no circumstances will you ever touch the petals of these orchids." She realized she was using a rather forceful voice, and she laughed at herself. "I must protect them, you know. You may touch something less valuable, perhaps. A flower growing outside, already exposed to the elements. An aster, or a dahlia. Perhaps a rose in its second bloom. And I do not mean to suggest that you could not tell which one was the plant and which the person."

She noticed he had not taken his eyes from her mouth. Goodness.

She continued her silly speech. "I believe that even without years of specific training as a botanist you ought to be able to find some differences."

He stood and took her hand in his. "Are there roses in this greenhouse?" Lucas asked, his voice soft.

She shook her head, feeling a shift in the air around them. When she answered, her voice came out quiet as well. "There are roses in the rose garden," she offered, as though he had never considered such a thing.

"If you do not object, I should like to put your idea to an experiment."

"My idea?" she echoed in a whisper. Had breathing ever been such an effort?

"The comparison. One thing like another. How can I know if it is a fair assessment unless I study them myself?" He looked down at their clasped hands and then back at her face.

She was very aware of her own heartbeat. With a great deal of air in her voice, she said, "As a student of science, Mr. Harding, I approve of your suggestion."

Holding hands, they walked out of the hothouse and to-ward the rose garden, their progress slowed by the fact that they stared into each other's faces far more often than they watched the path.

A low stone wall separated the rose garden from another one bordered by a formal hedge. Lucas led Hyacinth down the rows of roses, the bushes running slightly wild without the constant care of the gardeners. She told him the names of the ones she knew, and he nodded as if it mattered. They passed blooms of white and red and coral, Lucas glancing from Hyacinth's face to each bud and flower. He stopped her at a rosebush bursting with pink blooms.

Pointing, he asked, "What are these called?"

The ruffled edges of the open roses created a lovely shell

effect. "I do not know this variety. Perhaps you should name it," she said.

"The flower is exactly the same color as your mouth," he said, reaching for a rose and plucking an outer petal.

It was simply a statement. An observable fact. Why, then, did it take her breath away?

"Is it?" she asked, surprised at the effort it took to make a sound. How did he so easily stir her?

He held the petal up to her face, placing the fingers of his other hand ever so lightly near her chin, tilting her head toward the light of the afternoon sun. "I believe it is a perfect match," he said, drawing closer to her in his inspection. His voice grew even softer. "This rose should be named Hyacinth."

She could feel his breath on her face.

"I think you will find there is already a flower with that name," she said, her whisper carried to him on the light breeze.

"The best of them all," he murmured. "But do not try to distract me from my experiment."

He continued to hold the petal between his fingers, and without taking his eyes from her lips, he made a tiny circle with his thumb over the surface of the bloom. Slowly he raised his other hand, but instead of touching her mouth, he placed his fingers so lightly upon her neck that she wondered if it was perhaps a trick of the breeze. But as he moved his hand slowly, gently up the length of her neck, there was no question. Heat radiated from his tender touch as his fingers traveled the curve of her cheek.

Legs trembling, she wondered if she could continue to

stand, but even as the thought occurred to her, she felt herself leaning into his touch like buttercups tilting into the path of the sun. His finger, light as a breath, arrived at her mouth. He looked a request into her eyes, and she nodded once.

As his thumb traced her lower lip, her eyes fluttered closed. Was she floating? Was she even breathing? She felt his heartbeat through his hand, blood pulsing beneath his skin, life touching life. The flower petal he held brushed against her cheek, and she opened her eyes to see him gazing at her, adoration filling his eyes.

She reached for the petal, gently taking it from his fingers and holding it between her own. Carrying it to his mouth, she drew it across his lip, tracing the curve of his warm smile. "Do you feel that?" she asked.

He nodded, his breath a shudder.

Lifting herself upon her toes, she closed the last of the distance between them. "Is this different?" she whispered, brushing her lips across his.

He made a humming sound. "I think I have insufficient evidence. Do you mind if we try that again?"

She whispered her answer against his lips. "In the name of scientific discovery?"

"For the edification of poets," he said, and then they were not speaking any more.

❧

LAMENT

There is much to regret and much that I miss.
But the notion that is now and forever outside my reach,
The feeling I can never recover,
The most lost thing
Is
Hope.

CHAPTER 10

Hyacinth closed her bedroom door and leaned against it, imagining that Lucas stood opposite, his heart and hers beating in unison through the heavy wooden door. She pressed her hands to her cheeks, feeling the residual heat on her skin and reveling in the blissful memory of that sweet and surprising kiss.

How could it be that only a week ago, there was no Lucas Harding in her life? Every time she stepped into the greenhouse, she moved with the anticipation of when he would appear. Not only that, but with the expectation that he would be as delighted to see her as she was to see him.

Unfastening her skirt and changing it for a nightgown was the work of a few moments. She hung her working clothes in the wardrobe, pausing to run her hand over the soft, silky fabric of the one pretty dress she had brought with her to Ashthorne.

She pictured herself, hair shining and piled into a magnificent creation atop her head, looking lovely in a blue dinner dress that complemented her eyes, sitting across from Lucas at the enormous dining table in the great hall. In her fantasy, candles burned atop every available surface. Far more candles than would ever be called for. An absolute abundance of candles. And the table laden with platters of roast fowl, joints of meat, berries, jewel-bright carrots and beetroot, loaves in every shade of brown, pies, pastries, and cake after cake after cake.

She even thought she could hear the tinkling melody of a song played on a pianoforte accompanying the meal. What a delight to have such an imagination on nights like this. *Was* it imagination? It seemed she actually could hear the sound. But piano music . . . now? So late in the evening? Her mind must be swept away by her dream.

Well, nothing for it but to give in to the dream. More candlelight. More glances across the table. More music.

The idea of Mrs. Carter supplying and serving every last morsel of this imaginary feast marred the pleasure of the image, so Hyacinth simply conjured up a full kitchen and serving staff to go along with the sumptuous, fanciful meal. She sat on the edge of her bed, eyes closed, trying to bring scents to her mind to match the images. The pleasure of such imaginings was so great it felt practically painful.

Finally, she realized the pain was real, and she was, in fact, hungry. She sighed and pulled a wrapper around her shoulders. She would go into the kitchen and find something to eat. She took the taper out of its holder on her bedside table and made her way downstairs.

The hallway, vast and dark, felt different in the nighttime hours, more unnerving, more uncanny. And never more than tonight, when thought of strangers wandered through her imagination.

What had been recognizable in the light of day took on a new and unfamiliar potential, all too often sinister. Each doorway held a shadow as dark as the entrance to a cave. Every alcove and niche yawned with a depthless possibility. The ever-present breeze whistling out of each closed door was proof that even the thick stone walls could not keep the outside at bay.

Flickering candlelight did little to illuminate the long staircase, but even in the dark, Hyacinth found herself looking across to the north wing. Nothing. Of course there was nothing. She ran down the last few steps and across the foyer, the breeze she created scattering the small light from her candle in splashes.

She entered the kitchen, relieved to find the bowl of apples still on the sideboard. The kitchen fire was banked for the night, casting only the slightest reddish glow from the cinders, and she did not linger. Hurrying back to the stairs, she noticed her taper dripping a fine rivulet of wax toward her hand. She could stop and find a candlestick, but now that she had her apple, she wanted nothing more than to regain her bedroom and bury herself in blankets.

Then she saw the flicker of light across the entryway.

A single candle stood on the pianoforte in the music room, the feeble light of its flame barely reaching the hangings covering the room's windows.

But the room appeared empty, aside from the flickering candle. Hyacinth wandered closer, curious about the unattended fire, even such a small one. Why was the candle here?

And lit, when nobody was in the room? Had someone recently left?

Had Lucas been here tonight, his music somehow reaching her from across the house? Was it his song that had played in her fantasy?

But if it had been Lucas, why would he have left in a hurry, and when she had just crossed the entry hall? And Lucas would never leave a candle burning unattended.

She snuffed the candle and carried it with her, not wanting any of the soft wax to drip upon the surface of the piano. A candle in each hand, she turned back to the stairs. Her imagination rolled through one explanation after another, all of which were impossible. She really must get herself to bed.

As she began to mount the stairs, something white caught her eye, fluttering atop the north wing staircase in a gust of that same internal wind that deviled her own hallway. As Hyacinth looked directly at it, the flickering image seemed to disappear. She lowered her candle, removing it from her line of sight. After a blink, the image resolved itself into a figure, dressed in flowing white with a veil covering its face.

Hyacinth stilled, her breath coming in short, silent gasps. The figure turned. Hyacinth was unable to move, her feet rooted to the stairs. The outline of a woman brought to her mind the night of her arrival, when, from across the manor's approach, she had seen a figure silhouetted in a lighted window. The flickering of white at her bedroom door. The flowing image outside the hothouse. Here she was again.

Her throat closed around the cry that rose in her chest, but even then, Hyacinth was unsure if her involuntary call was meant to beckon the figure or send it away. Not taking her eyes off the fluttering white figure, she forced her feet to move from the base of the south staircase toward the forbidden north steps.

"Wait," Hyacinth called, the word coming out strangled. She tried again. "Wait, please."

The figure stilled.

At the foot of the north stairs, Hyacinth stopped for a beat, thoughts of Mrs. Carter's rules halting her. Then, eyes focused on the white form atop the staircase, she took the steps, one by one.

The figure remained still, as if it was watching her, until Hyacinth reached the middle of the staircase. Without a sound, it turned and glided down the hall. Faster than Hyacinth's upward approach, it was gone. This was no ordinary woman. Was she even human?

Who could move like that? Hide so effortlessly?

Hyacinth could see no sign of the figure. It either disappeared into a room, or simply disappeared. But that was impossible, both to believe and to accept.

Stepping now into the forbidden north hallway, she tried the knob of the first door. Locked. The second was locked as well. On she went, trying each door on one side of the vast hallway and then the other. Each door was sealed, just as Mrs. Carter had said. Hyacinth knew she could open the doors with a bit of time and a few hairpins, but somehow, the spectral figure had accomplished the same without effort.

She felt certain she now knew what she had pursued. Behind one of those doors was a ghost. A spirit. A specter.

"Hello?" Hyacinth called.

There was no response. Not even a breath of answer.

"I'd like to speak with you," she said. "Please."

Who could the spirit be? And then she remembered what Lucas had told her about his cousin, Mrs. Carter's daughter who had passed away from a tragic illness.

"Rosa?" she called into the hallway.

She heard a gasp. "How do you know that name?" The voice that spoke was crackly with disuse.

"Is it you?" Hyacinth asked, nearing the door from which the voice came. "Rosa?"

The shuddering voice whispered from behind the wood. "I have waited a long time for someone to speak that name to me."

"I am very happy to speak with you," Hyacinth said, her excitement barely kept within control. Was she actually having a conversation with a ghost? This was more than she could have dreamed. "May I stay?"

The voice came through the door in a whisper. "This is a lonely house."

"It is," Hyacinth said. "But you have a friend here now, if you'll have me."

Was that a sob?

Hyacinth racked her brain for any ghost lore she could call on. She remembered hearing something about unfinished business. "Is there something you need?"

"He's looking for me," she said. "He thinks I have something he needs."

That was not at all what she expected to hear. Baffled, Hyacinth asked, "Who?"

There was no reply, but the sob turned to a low wail,

strangely reminiscent of the sound of wind through the stones.

Hyacinth heard a door slam and startled. Was it Mrs. Carter, awakened from her sleep?

"I must go, but I hope I can speak with you again," she said. Without waiting to hear another word from the ghost, Hyacinth ran along the hall, down the stairs, back up the twin staircase, and along the south hallway to her room, delicious shivers running along her arms.

Ashthorne Hall held more secrets than it was possible to believe.

LAMENT

If only.

If only I could show myself to her, could make a friend of this girl.

She seems to have no fear, but one look at my wreck of a face and she would run away and never come back.

The ruin will never end. Illness and death were not enough.

This curse demands more and more.

Far more than I have strength to give.

CHAPTER 11

When Hyacinth woke the next morning, she wondered if the whole encounter had been a dream. But then she saw the second candle on her table, the one she'd lifted from the top of the piano and carried up to her room.

Proof. Evidence that she'd been in the entry hall, found the candle burning in the music room, and then followed that flitting, gauzy figure up the forbidden staircase.

And she'd spoken with the spirit. Called her by name. Heard her ruined voice. Held a real conversation.

It was true, wasn't it? Hyacinth did not want to doubt her experience, but now, in the light of morning, her rational mind attempted to list all the reasons it couldn't have happened.

For a person in the habit of depending on facts, Hyacinth Bell ignored rationality. Fantasy and mysticism were much more fun.

As she dressed for the day, she felt a rush of excitement at the idea of sharing the upper floor of the manor with a specter. Not to mention her newfound ability to unlock the forbidden doors through the servants' staircase. Nothing at Ashthorne was hidden from her now.

What would Lucas say?

Her smile grew wide at the realization that he was the next destination of her thoughts. She wondered if he had woken this morning thinking of her.

Though eager to get into the orchid house as quickly as possible, Hyacinth took a moment to ensure that her plaited hair was pinned up in a way that emphasized her neck. Remembering the touch of Lucas's whisper-soft fingers against the skin just above the collar of her blouse gave her another thrill strong enough to heat her cheeks.

Orchids and ghosts and romance. What more could any woman want? Hyacinth felt like a character in a novel, and nothing could please her more.

In the kitchen, the basket of fruit sat beside the bread platter. And a folded sheet of paper, addressed to her.

Miss Hyacinth Bell, Gatherer of Evidence.

She unfolded the paper and found a note written in a tidy hand.

Dear Miss Bell,

I hope you slept well. I certainly did, content with dreams and memories that will become dreams.

Would you do me the honor of joining me for a picnic this evening? If it is agreeable to you, I shall meet you at the orchid house at five o'clock.

If you are not inclined to join me, I will need to reexamine evidence I have gathered.

Yours,

Lucas

Yours. What a lovely word.

Hyacinth tucked the note into her pocket and held on to her smile all day.

Any attempt to ignore time is foolish, and Hyacinth never noticed its slow passage more than that day. She felt the rays of the sun in every angle as it moved across the sky, the beams falling through the glass of the orchid house from the bright morning east, from noon's sunshine above, and in the leaning of the afternoon light from the west.

When she heard the door swing open, she closed her notebook, straightened the blue ribbon on Eleanor's stake, and peeled off her gloves as Lucas entered.

As a botanist, Hyacinth knew the purpose of all the parts of a plant, how each root and leaf and bloom worked together, the synchrony of function to grow and regrow, either from season to season or by dropping new seeds. People mostly noticed the blossoms, but through her studies, Hyacinth had grown to appreciate the magic of the less obvious parts. Of course, she adored a pretty petal as much as anyone, but that was not all a plant had to offer.

She wondered which of the elements that made up Lucas Harding was the blossom. Which element did others notice first? His charming manners? His confident presence? The way that lock of hair tumbled across his forehead, giving a hint of the boy he once was? Hyacinth felt sure it must be his smile, the one he was giving her now, that spoke of an open delight at being near her.

An answering smile covered her own face.

Lucas reached for her hand, pressed a kiss into her fingers, and asked if she was finished with her work.

She wanted to tell him about the ghost of his cousin, to ask if he, too, had seen her. But something told her that was a discussion for a different time. Perhaps she needed to let him bring Rosa into the conversation on his own.

"I have done what I can for now and will give the orchids the rest of the day to complete their tasks," she said. "Sometimes it's best to let the plants do the work."

Oh, how quickly she had grown to love the sound of his laugh. What might she say next to elicit that laugh again?

He escorted her out of the orchid house and along one of the garden walks, a basket swinging in one of his hands. They passed through a formal garden and then turned toward the forested hill.

She held his arm as he told her more stories, history of the manor, legends of families long past who made life either simple or difficult for the tenant farmers or the villagers. Some of his stories sounded like the mythology that must be attached to every prominent house in the kingdom.

She loved the sound of his voice and wished that she could tell him so. As that felt far too forward, she told him another true thing. "I love hearing you tell of the history of Ashthorne."

Lucas drew her closer with a movement of his arm. "It's not all history. There's plenty of fable and folklore. Some of the stories can't be true. Like the pirate tales."

Hyacinth remembered Mr. Gardner and James had both spoken about pirates and ghosts and was intrigued. "Can't they?" she prompted, hoping he would tell more.

He was happy to oblige, tucking her arm even more tightly within his grasp as they walked along the wooded path. "I suppose some of them had to be facts once, but so many stories grew wildly from simple events that none of the tales are trustworthy anymore. Cornwall coast legends are steeped in stories of shipwrecks, chests of gold and jewels lost and found, intrigue and deception. Daring rescues and hidden fortunes tucked into cliffside caves. Those kinds of stories sparked my imagination as a little boy."

"I loved those kinds of stories too," she said. "I still do."

They approached a partially obscured stone-pillared folly, half of which glowed in the afternoon sun while the other half had been swallowed by the encroaching forest. The Grecian-style circular platform seemed to serve no logical purpose other than to look charming in the landscape, which, Hyacinth decided, it did.

"I love the wildness at the edges of the property. If I could go back in time and thank the original Ashthorne occupants for planting such an abundance of trees, I would. Seeing the overgrowth, it's hard to believe they didn't spring up naturally. When I think how close these trees are to the barren moors, I want to reach out and touch each one. To help it stand up against the wind. To tell it to keep growing strong. I know they don't need my help, but I do love to know they grow here despite the inhospitable landscape."

"You are a delight," he murmured, his eyes meeting hers, and she did not dare respond as she felt no more in control of her words than she was of her heartbeat. Just as her pulse ran wild, she knew her words would too.

They walked again down the cliffside stone steps, Lucas guiding her gently once they reached the high tide marks. "The rocks get slippery here," he reminded her. "Even when the tide's been out for hours, some of these stones never seem to dry."

When they arrived at the small beach, Lucas walked to the water's edge and then back. "I think we have plenty of time to eat before the water comes too close," he said.

"You don't need to worry about my escape. I'm an excellent runner," Hyacinth answered. "Not to mention swimmer."

Lucas shook his head, and his smile vanished. When he spoke, his voice was low and serious. "High tide in this bay is treacherous. The waves come up against the rocks in a terrifying roar. And the undertow is powerful. Please, Hyacinth. Don't swim here."

Startled at his vehement response to her joke, she shook her head. "I wouldn't dream of it. I was being silly. I'm sorry I upset you."

With a sigh, Lucas shook his head. "You need not apologize. I often let my mind move from simple conversations to the worst possible outcomes. I do not mean to ruin your happiness with my occasional gloom."

Hyacinth thought of other conversations they'd had in the last few days, times when Lucas seemed to dip into a darker mood. She knew some people tended toward melancholy, but she did not feel this was something he ought to blame himself for.

Hyacinth shook her head and smiled at Lucas. "You do not need to apologize for how you feel. And I appreciate that you look out for my safety here where you know the dangers so much better than I do."

However, to save him from any additional pain, she

would remove from her mind thoughts of teasing him with her pretended bravery. He did not appreciate such jests, and so she gathered all such thoughts together and then swirled them in her mind, collecting them so she could remove them. A good use of her thought-trick if it made Lucas feel better.

Hyacinth was even more certain it would not be wise to mention her spectral visit last night. Lucas would not be as excited by the events as she was. He might see Rosa's appearance as another possible danger.

She would keep that to herself until he appeared more interested in such adventures.

Lucas tilted his head to the right and left as if shaking a weight from his neck. He took a breath and found his smile again. She watched in appreciation as he removed his jacket from his broad shoulders and placed it on the ground.

"Will you be comfortable here?" he asked, gesturing for her to sit.

She adored the question. Not "Will you be useful?" Not "Will you be important?" He did not expect her to produce anything, but simply to enjoy a moment.

Her heart found its rhythm again as she watched him un-pack the basket Mrs. Carter surely prepared for them. He laid a cloth down, placed a plate filled with bread and cheese upon it, and removed two small crockery jars. He opened the lids, and she saw that one held butter and the other, jewel-bright fruit preserves. A bowl containing cold roast chicken appeared next, and last, a pair of linen napkins. He set about preparing a plate for her, and she adored the way he carefully served each item, placing it just so, glancing her way to reassure himself he was doing it to her satisfaction.

She could think of very few things that might bring her more satisfaction right now.

They ate and talked, comparing stories of childhood escapades as well as their more recent wishes and dreams.

"If you could meet one famous person, who would it be?" Lucas asked her.

"Do you know Mr. Darwin?"

"Not personally."

Hyacinth laughed. "I mean, are you aware of the work of Charles Darwin? He published a book several years ago about the variety of orchids' shapes and colors. He believes that certain flowers have developed particular patterns to attract specific pollinators."

Lucas buttered another slice of bread and put it on her plate. "Do you mean that one kind of bee will love one kind of orchid?"

She nodded. "I hear the doubt in your voice, and you're in good company. Many people argue with Darwin's findings, but no one has yet proven him wrong. It is fascinating to think that certain types of orchids grow best when an insect transfers pollen from one plant to another."

It occurred to Hyacinth that she was discussing reproduction with a man who was not a scientist, and she quickly turned the conversation. "So I would love to meet Mr. Darwin. How about you? Whom would you like to meet?"

He rubbed the back of his neck. "Would you think me silly if I said I'd like to meet the queen?" he asked.

"Not silly at all. I believe her to be a very impressive person."

He nodded. "I know people are bound to tell either the

most positive or the most negative stories about the monarchy, but she seems to be a woman who knows something about everything. I'd like to learn about everything as well."

"Perhaps the four of us could spend an evening together. Share a meal. Trade philosophies," Hyacinth said, nodding to underscore what a very reasonable idea such a gathering might be.

"A very good notion," Lucas said, echoing Hyacinth's pretended seriousness. "Mr. Darwin and Queen Victoria would leave the meeting enriched by our contributions."

"Naturally," she agreed. She believed she would agree with anything he said as long as he kept smiling at her.

When the food was eaten and the dishes replaced in the basket, they looked up at the cliff wall. From this angle, they could not see the house. Lucas pointed out the parts of the property visible from the crescent of sand, and he counted holes in the cliff that might be caves. They imagined what creatures might live within those caves until sitting on the sand became uncomfortable for Hyacinth. Lucas saw her shifting and jumped to his feet. Taking her hands, he helped her stand, then gathered his coat.

He brushed sand from his jacket and the picnic cloth. Hyacinth loved watching him perform these small services for her. She smiled at him. "Thank you for bringing me here. It's a lovely place for us to have spent a lovely evening."

He smiled and took her hand. "Do you wish to return to the manor already? Because we have not yet had our dance."

"Dance?" she asked, wondering if she misheard him.

"Oh, if you insist," he said, turning her clarification into an invitation. "But we don't have long. The tide is coming in soon."

She laughed as he took her by the hand and turned her in a circle on the diminishing crescent of sand.

Could he see how dizzy his gaze made her? Did he know that she'd imagined dancing with him?

"There is no music," she said, a hint of disappointment coloring her voice.

Pulling her close, he looked into her eyes and whispered, "I brought the music with me."

Unable to look away from his gaze, she wondered what kind of music he'd managed to transport in a picnic basket. Lucas Harding wrapped an arm around Hyacinth's back and began to hum in her ear. As they spun in time to his song, Hyacinth felt the surroundings go fuzzy around her as she remained focused solely on the man who held her and the accompaniment of the ocean's waves.

How was it possible that she could have a moment like this? What had she ever done to deserve such happiness? She clasped her hand tightly with his and fell into the music, the movement, and his gaze.

❧

LAMENT

I see them there, walking hand in hand and holding each other tight.

No one will ever touch me that way again.

Some losses cannot be recovered, and some damage cannot be undone.

I thought I understood loss and grief,

But each new day I find another way I've lost myself.

CHAPTER 12

The idea of saying good night had never struck Hyacinth as a delicious event. But then, she had never before had a Lucas Harding to say good night to.

She felt like she might burst out of her skin. Like sitting still was impossible. Like she was filled with starlight and music. She might have been embarrassed at the spin and the happy squeal she made as she closed the door to her room, but no one was there to witness it but Eleanor. Hyacinth had stopped into the orchid house to bring her favorite flower inside for the night.

"Dearest," she said, feeling breathless and giddy. "Our situation here at Ashthorne would be perfect even if you were the only orchid I ever saw."

Hyacinth cleaned the sand from her skirts and shoes, humming Lucas's song as she worked.

"Eleanor," Hyacinth said, lifting her beloved orchid and holding her head close to the flower's bloom, "I believe I've fallen for Mr. Lucas Harding."

Was it the confession or simply saying his name aloud

that made Hyacinth smile? She tried speaking the sentence a few more times but was unable to make a distinction between possible causes.

Very well, she thought. *I'll replicate the experiment as often as possible.*

As the evening's silence fell over the manor, she placed Eleanor's pot carefully on the dressing table and wrapped herself in her shawl. "Good night, dearest," she said to the orchid. "Time for me to open a few closed doors." With a candle and two matches in her hand, she closed the door quietly behind her.

As she tiptoed down the steps of the grand staircase, she wondered how careful she needed to be. Would Mrs. Carter watch from a corner of the entryway to see if Hyacinth disobeyed her rules?

"Really," Hyacinth murmured to herself, "the woman is far too busy to sit in darkness trying to catch me out." Even so, she did not light her candle as she moved from the south staircase to the north.

A newly familiar sense of adventure accompanied her as she walked up the forbidden staircase, made her way to the second door on the right, and pulled a pin from her hair. With practiced motion, she brought the pin toward the mechanism, only to have the door open under her touch. It was unlocked.

How strange. Would Mrs. Carter have neglected to lock this door after going inside? And what might she have needed from within the room?

Hyacinth stepped in and pulled the door closed behind her. With a strike of the match on the door's wooden molding, a spark ignited, and she lit her candle, eager to explore the room.

She sucked in a gasp. This was not a room Mrs. Carter had entered and left unlocked. This was chaos. She could barely make sense of what lay before her. Holland covers were pulled from the furnishings and cast on the floor. Framed paintings hung at precarious angles. An armoire was pulled open, drawers emptied and discarded. Instead of the pile of boxes she'd seen in the other room, there was a tumbled mess of books, papers, and small decorative items. It looked as if someone had pulled the crates down, searching for something inside.

This could not be the work of Mrs. Carter. If she needed to find a book or a document, she would move methodically through the boxes instead of creating messes she'd need to clear up herself.

As Hyacinth moved deeper into the room, she noticed a familiar but misplaced lingering smell of tobacco smoke.

Had the man who entered her bedroom been in the house again tonight? In this very room? The thought made her skin crawl. If he'd caused this destruction, what was he looking for?

Hyacinth picked up a few of the clothes from the pile on the floor. Woolens. Thick stockings. Winter wear. Things the family would not need for their new life in the tropics. But nothing an intruder would be interested in. She doubted the prowler was hoping to find a child's jumper.

And she felt certain he was looking for something.

But what?

She turned slowly around the tumbled room, holding her

candle out in front of her, searching for understanding. Data. Information.

Her mind raced through possibilities, and she felt a shiver of surprise when a new thought occurred to her. Could a ghost make a mess like this?

Had Rosa Carter assaulted the room in this way? And if so, why?

What could a spirit gain by such destruction? Was she seeking the notice of her mother, perhaps? For at some point, Mrs. Carter would enter and see this disaster.

Hyacinth's mind took hold of this hypothesis, and she knew she had to test it.

Was there a method to this ruin? Did it continue in other rooms?

She moved to leave, to check the state of the next room, and then saw a lone sheet of paper on the floor by the door. She had not noticed it when she had come in, surprised as she was by the state of the room. Seeing it now, she wondered if the message was meant for her.

Large, blocky letters spelled out the words, "Speak to no one."

Despite her tendency to ignore commands, Hyacinth shuddered as she read the warning. She lifted the paper from the ground, turning it over. She found nothing to explain the instruction. Speak to no one about what?

Had Rosa managed to write this message? Could a spirit hold a pencil?

Again, Hyacinth wished she knew more ghost lore.

Closing the door softly behind her, Hyacinth stepped

out into the dark hallway. Midway down the north wing, she stopped walking and called in a tentative voice. "Rosa?"

When she realized she was straining to listen for any sound of supernatural movement, Hyacinth almost laughed. What did she expect? The rustling of a ghostly gown? Rosa hadn't made noise before. Except for her voice.

She called again. "Rosa? Are you here? It's Hyacinth."

We're both flowers, she realized.

Would she appear if Hyacinth said she needed her? She believed so. Admittedly, Hyacinth had no evidence to support such an impression, but she had an idea that spirits lingered because they still had work to do. Unfinished business.

Maybe she could use this. "Rosa, I have a question. Can you help me?"

She moved farther down the hall, calling softly.

"If you help me, I will be able to help you," she said.

Nothing answered. When she was outside the door through which she'd spoken to the ghost before, Hyacinth asked her question again.

"There is so much I don't know. I believe you can see more than I see in this house. Can you help me understand?"

There. A rustling behind the door.

"Can you let me inside? May I open the door?"

Hyacinth waited for a reply but heard nothing. She ought not invade the privacy of this spirit, so she wouldn't push her way in. But neither would she leave.

"Why must you be a secret?"

Was that a sigh?

Hyacinth stopped. Waited.

After a long pause, the raspy, ravaged voice spoke. "Safer this way."

"Safer for whom?" Hyacinth asked.

"All of us. Everyone."

"Is there danger here, then?"

Perhaps Rosa knew about the man. Perhaps she feared his presence. If so, she did not admit it to Hyacinth.

"Can you tell me if someone has been prowling through the manor? Someone who doesn't belong here?"

Another long pause. Hyacinth would wait for her answer.

"Do you or I belong here?" The voice spoke quietly. Sadly.

Was this a test? Did she need to prove something to Rosa's ghost?

"Of course we do. I was invited to come. And you followed your family. At least, that's how it seems. Did you come here after your mother took over the housekeeper job this summer?"

She might be asking too much, she knew.

"I can't talk about that," the voice said, but it sounded closer to the door. "Too much must remain secret. Please go to your room. I fear you're not safe wandering the manor like this."

"I'm not afraid," Hyacinth said, but the tapered candle trembled in her hands. "Who else walks these halls?"

No answer.

"Is he looking for me? I think he's been in my room."

A moan.

"Don't worry. No one will hurt me. I'll be safe."

A ragged whisper came through the door. "Please go to your room. And lock the door."

"Do you go into my room as well?" Hyacinth asked. She didn't want the ghost to feel threatened, so she added, "You are welcome there."

Hyacinth listened closely, her ear pressed to the door. She heard a sound of assent.

Suddenly she thought of a flower. A seashell. Strawberries in a pewter bowl. "Have you left me gifts?"

"I am glad to share this house with you."

It wasn't an answer, exactly, but Hyacinth understood. Those small items left on her nightstand, the figure in the hall, the piano music in the night, the flicker of white at her door and at the hothouse—it was all Rosa.

"I am glad as well."

"But now you must go," the voice said faintly. "Please. Lock your door and sleep."

Hyacinth was unlikely to sleep any time soon, but she had no intention of upsetting the ghost. "If you wish it," she said. "Good night, Rosa."

She heard a whispered echo in return. "Good night, Rosa."

That was strange. Perhaps she repeated Hyacinth's farewell because it had been so long since anyone had spoken to her. Maybe she had missed conversation, the sound of her own name. Hyacinth laid her hand on the door, then returned, albeit unwillingly, to her room.

As she lay in bed waiting for sleep to find her, she thought of mentioning Rosa during a conversation with Lucas. Or with Mrs. Carter. It seemed only fair that if she could see the ghost of someone they loved, they ought to be able to as well.

She drifted off with a smile, considering how sweet it would be for her to have another chance to speak to her mother. Mrs. Carter must feel the same way about the ghost of her girl.

One more morning of sunshine and Hyacinth might stop believing in ghosts altogether. Good thing she had constant proof on her side.

Hyacinth spent the day debating how to speak to Lucas about her visits with Rosa's ghost. Could she simply ask him if he had seen her? Or must she be more delicate? He could be helpful in increasing her own understanding of Rosa's life and death. In whatever way she chose to do it, however, she knew she must tell him about the spirit in the halls of Ashthorne.

This was not simply a haunting in an old manor house. Not any ghost from a story. She was his cousin. Even though Rosa seemed sure she must remain a secret, she could not intend to hide from her family.

And Hyacinth must tell Lucas a man moved through the house. He needed to know.

Hyacinth wondered if she had misread the note she found on the ransacked room's floor. She knew the words, of course, but might they have come from the prowler instead of the spirit?

She must speak to Lucas about all of it, despite the warnings.

But when he met her on the path through the grove that afternoon, he seemed unaware of the need for investigation or the revelation of secrets.

"Ah, Miss Hyacinth Bell, you are the best part of my day by far. The sight of you is enough to turn around even the most discouraging mood."

The smile that bloomed across his face thrilled her more than the blossoming of the most precious flower.

"Has your work been difficult today?" she asked.

He kept his smile, though she could see a strain behind it. "I've had my fill of troubles, right to the top. There is room for no more." He shook his head playfully. "I will hear nothing but happiness today, thank you."

After he had been so open with her about the bouts of darkness that clouded his heart and mind, how could she trouble him with her concerns?

Of course, they were his concerns as well, or they soon would be.

But seeing him so eager for her company and ready to be pleased, she knew her worries could wait.

Lucas took her arm. "How are the orchids faring today?"

She pushed her anxious thoughts from her mind with effort. "Everything in this place feels bigger and stronger than I expected," she said.

"I can explain that," he said. "We credit it to fresh Cornish breezes and love."

Was it so simple for him to speak the word "love"? Could she do the same? "Breezes and love, is it? I don't believe those are listed in any of the gardening articles I've read lately."

"New information is always presenting itself," Lucas said.

Oh, how she adored his smile.

"And your evidence?" she asked, using the question as an excuse to study his face.

Tightening his arm around her, he asked, "Are you trying to make a scientist of me? I assure you, I have loads of evidence. Look at the bloom in your cheeks. You might be part flower for how well you're growing here in the west."

She nodded. "Right. With the breezes. And the love."

He leaned close to her ear. "If our experiment requires us to change a variable, it must be the breezes. For there is no chance now that we can test anything without the love. I fear it's no longer variable. What do you call the parts that don't change?"

Why was breathing such a challenge? "Constants," she said, the word coming out on a whisper of air.

"Ah, constant. Indeed. I shall be exceedingly constant."

The way he looked at her made her believe he truly would be.

He continued, "But perhaps we need more data. I think the best results come with repetition of the experiment. Are you willing to make another trial? For the sake of science?"

"Are we still discussing flowers?" she asked, though she knew the answer.

"Would you be sorry if we were not?" His question came with a tilt of his head and a very suggestive smile.

"To repeat our previous experiment? I would not be sorry in the least. We must gather all the evidence we can. For science."

Additional evidence was inconclusive, but, undaunted, they continued to investigate.

LAMENT

When I remember my life, how I moved through the world
before it all changed,
    I cannot hear laughter.
    I cannot smell delicious aromas of the city.
    I cannot see the smiling eyes of my dearest friend.
    I remember the fear.
    The rot.
    The crying.
    The stink of disease.
    I remember the dread, and it will not leave me.
    How can I teach myself to see and hear and recall
    What once was beautiful?
    I must borrow such feelings from those who still live in the
world.

CHAPTER 13

They made their way to the house, arm in arm, and sat in the green-painted morning room.

"Is this not rebellious of us?" Hyacinth asked. "Morning rooms in the afternoon?"

Lucas said, "I prefer to think of it as avoiding falling into the rut of the expected." He still watched her with his eyes aslant and his smile playing at the corner of his mouth. That beautiful mouth.

"Ah, you are rather unpredictable, are you not?" she said.

He leaned over and kissed her. "You did not see that coming, did you?"

Laughing, she said, "Perhaps I did not expect it. But I did hope."

"Anything that you wish, my dear." He kissed her again.

He sat across a small table from her, and she wondered if this was the time to bring up the prowler. And Rosa.

But it was not to be, for Lucas introduced yet another interesting topic when he said, "I believe I told you about my sister."

Ah, yes. That would do.

"I believe you mentioned she exists. That is not the same thing as telling me about her." Hyacinth hoped the smile she sent him took the sting out of her criticism.

He nodded. "I am protective of her," he said simply. "But she would like to be known to you." He looked down at the table and then back at her. The way he gazed at her, as if he needed to shield his eyes from her radiance, warmed her from the inside out.

"She has heard of me?" Hyacinth felt pleased as well as surprised. "How can that be?"

Lucas ducked his head and then grinned bashfully. "I wrote to her about you. I may have expressed my opinion that you had become important to me."

Hyacinth reveled in such a sweet admission.

"And she responded?"

"She did. I correspond with her nearly every day."

"That is lovely. Tell me about her," she said, wishing that instead, she could ask him exactly what he had told his sister about her. About his impression of her, and about their growing attachment.

"Polly is three years older than I. When I was a baby, she would carry me about, dropping me only infrequently."

Hyacinth laughed.

He continued. "As we grew, she took care to see that I did nothing to mar her reputation as the perfect elder sister. Or rather, when I did, she would require my penance."

"I should dearly like to hear of your childhood transgressions," Hyacinth said, "but that can wait. Carry on." She sat back and placed her hands on the table in front of her.

Lucas reached out his own hand and touched the edge of her wrist with one finger. She wondered if she could continue to pay attention to his words given such a sweet distraction.

As it happened, she was equally interested in his story and his touch.

"We were fast friends. When our mother died, Polly took her place in many ways, teaching me, comforting me, and loving me."

It was Hyacinth's experience that a mother's role was more than simply the sweet parts. "And reprimanding you?"

He nodded. "When necessary." Then he gave her a grin. "But I believe I outgrew many of my worst habits by that time."

Hyacinth wished she could ask him about his tendencies toward childhood wickedness, but she let him guide the conversation.

"Our father's death followed not long after our mother's, and Polly and I were left to make our own way. With the help of local solicitors, I sold my father's farm, as I told you, and found my way to school. After discharging family debts, there was not enough money for us to live comfortably, at least not indefinitely, so Polly and I decided to save what we could, and we each sought work as we were able. Polly found a place in London, working in a factory with our cousin Rosa."

Ah, Rosa—the very person Hyacinth had been wondering about for days. But she knew it would be rude to change the topic of their conversation and press Lucas for information, no matter how much she wanted it. Hyacinth bit her lip to stop herself asking for every fascinating detail about Rosa's life, but she found it almost impossible to sit and wait.

How could she ever exercise patience about a subject that had become so absorbing? Rosa was constantly on her mind.

But if he told stories about Polly and Rosa together, she would learn much about Rosa's history. She wanted to know all about their work, where the girls lived, and what they did in their hours outside their employment. And, of course, what had happened to Rosa in the end. She felt the strain of keeping her questions contained, and in her effort, she missed several sentences of Lucas's story.

She realized that, in her distraction, she might be ignoring exactly the parts of the tale she most desired, so she refocused her attention on his words.

"When Aunt Ellen alerted me to this caretaker position, we all agreed it would be a wonderful job for me to hold for the duration of the Whitbeck family's stay in India."

It was the most information Lucas had offered her at once about his past or his family. Hyacinth would have loved to hear more, but when he said, "Would you be willing to write to my sister?" Hyacinth knew his happiness depended on her answer.

"I shall begin today," she said. "This moment, if you wish it."

He leaned across the table and grasped both her hands in his. "I cannot tell you how glad this makes me. Polly has always been so very good to me, and I can think of nothing I would love more than for the two of you to be . . . known to each other," he finished after a pause.

Hyacinth wondered if he had meant to say something different in that small hesitation.

Lucas gathered paper, pen, and ink, placing them before her on the table, his smile growing wider every moment.

"How can I compose a letter with you hovering over my shoulder?" she asked, teasing him. "Here, sit beside me. But look away from the letter. I'm sure to make an inkblot if you're watching."

"I won't look at the paper," he said, and when she saw the way he gazed at her face, she believed him.

She dipped her pen and began to write.

Dear Miss Harding,

I have recently had the privilege of becoming acquainted with your brother. In fact, I have known him nearly a week and have decided he is quite the most charming man on this estate. This may come as a surprise to you, seeing as you have known him all his life and he assures me he was not always as agreeable as he is now, but you should know he credits you with every good character trait he has developed. And as there are no other men here, he must always win every competition of affability at Ashthorne.

Mr. Harding assures me that you are prepared to become my friend. If this is so, I must beg your agreement to a small proposal. For today's letter, I shall tell you one thing I hope for, one thing I fear, and one thing of which I am proud. If you agree, I should love to hear the same from you.

First, my hope. I wish to live to see the development of medicines that will prevent diseases. Ever since I learned that Dr. Jenner discovered vaccines that could stop the spread of smallpox, I have longed to see human disease eradicated. I know such a thing must seem impossible, but centuries ago, a Chinese monk believed that snake venom could not possibly cure snakebite. But behold! I should like to live to see the disappearance of tuberculosis, of influenza, of cholera. There is much to learn. We live in such an exciting age where every year seems to bring scientific improvements. Imagine a world without illness. This is my hope.

Often I pretend I am fearless, but in fact, I am not. There are some things I cannot bear even to think about, and one of those is monkeys. Yes. Monkeys. Years and years ago, I saw a monkey in a menagerie. It hung upon the edge of its cage and shrieked at me. I had a recurring nightmare throughout my childhood in which that monkey bared its terrifying teeth and shouted commands to me, but I could never understand them and so I never obeyed. He continued to scream as I stood there with tears rolling down my cheeks. Waking from those dreams left me shaking and terrified, and I have been afraid of monkeys ever since.

And now to run the risk of seeming self-important, I shall tell you something that makes me proud. I was educated in the care of certain tropical flowers. With my training, I have become something of an expert in orchids, and my abilities with these flowers has allowed me to meet interesting people, to study and regenerate several important collections, and to accept employment at Ashthorne, which has led me eventually to form an acquaintance with you.

If a reply to this silly note is in your power and your interest, I would be delighted to learn something of your own hopes, fears, and satisfactions.

In the meantime, I shall endeavor to amuse myself in this glorious, spacious house, the inhabitants of which include myself and your own Mrs. Carter.

And possibly a ghost.

Sincerely,

Hyacinth Bell

Hyacinth folded the paper in half and made a quick sketch of a vanda orchid on the blank side. When the drawing satisfied her, she passed the letter to Lucas.

"Would you care to seal it?" he asked.

"There is no need. You can combine it with your own and send them together."

Lucas smiled and held the letter carefully in his hands.

"Where in London is Miss Harding?" Hyacinth asked.

Lucas looked startled. "Why do you ask?"

"Because I do not know, and I always like to know everything there is to know."

"And how do you come along in that endeavor?" he asked.

"Bit by bit," she answered with a quirk of an eyebrow. "Especially when my direct questions are answered. Is she still staying in London?"

He shook his head. "My sister is living outside London. She should receive your letter tomorrow. Now I ought to write to her as well."

"Would you like me to sit next to you and tap my fingers upon the table as you write?" she asked.

He shook his head, bewildered. "No. Why would I want that?"

She grinned. "I thought perhaps that is how people from this county attend their friends who are writing, for that is what you did while I was writing my letter to your sister."

"Did I? I felt nervous about asking you to correspond with her. I dearly wish the two of you to be friends." He gave a quiet laugh. "How rude of me. I must have made that experience awful for you. I apologize."

Hyacinth shook her head, hoping Lucas would not fall into a dark moment. "That is unnecessary, I assure you. I will slowly unfold to you my small habits that will exasperate and alarm you. You have simply spared me the worry that I would need to be the first. So, in fact, I thank you."

"In that case, it is my pleasure." Lucas turned her letter round and round in his hands.

Hyacinth realized he was still nervous. It was clear he wanted very much for her to love his sister, and for his sister to love her back. Hyacinth was pleased, for it was not difficult to imagine why such a thing would matter to him.

He traced the lines of the flower she had sketched on the letter. "Perhaps you might draw me a picture while I write," he said.

"I am no artist," she countered.

He cleared his throat. "I have evidence to the contrary," he said, tilting the letter in her direction and indicating her work.

"Oh, that. Well, I can produce serviceable flower illustrations. But I cannot draw a horse without it resembling a dog, and were I to attempt to take your likeness, you should never forgive me. You might end up looking like a toad. Or an oxcart. Or a gargoyle."

She was being modest; her renderings were not masterful, but she was proficient at drawing. She enjoyed making him smile, though, so she thought she could be forgiven for a little falsehood.

"Do I naturally resemble those things?" he asked, with half a smile, setting down her letter and picking up the pen and a fresh piece of paper.

She shook her head. "None at all."

Her mind flooded with images of paintings and sculptures of gods and angels, and she felt her cheeks flush. "But I cannot draw any of the things you do resemble, either. So I would rather not attempt any portraiture." She hoped her playfulness did not offend him.

"I had no intention of you drawing a portrait of me. But perhaps a dog that looks like a horse." He passed her another sheet of paper. "Your mind moves in strange and interesting ways, Miss Bell," he said. "I am enjoying learning the workings of your brain."

She took the paper and ran her finger along the edge. "I am afraid it is not my brain so much as my disposition to say whatever comes to my mind. It is a common failing in the Bell family, I fear. My father is forever speaking his opinion."

Lucas set down his pen and paper. "Tell me," he prompted.

"After my mother died, my father began taking me with him as he made visits to his friends and their manors' farms. Another man might have left me with a governess, but I believe my father would have been lonely without me. He and my mother had always taught me, and so he continued to teach me, but instead of learning from books, I learned by watching him. He was most fond of farm chemistry and fertilizers, and much of his work benefits my own. As I learned at his side, he regularly questioned accepted scientific standards."

"He disagreed with professionals?"

"Constantly." She could not keep the pride from her voice. "He taught me the difference between knowing something because someone tells me it is true and knowing something because I discover it is true."

"That seems to be a very good aptitude to develop when you wish to work as a scientist," Lucas said.

She loved how he understood her.

"I believe it is an important skill for all people to learn, regardless of profession. It seems to me that the mark of a contributing member of society is the ability to learn and understand. One ought not to be at the mercy of another's information."

Lucas nodded.

"He also taught me the importance of shedding opinions when they're proven wrong. This has been a difficult thing to learn, but it's one of the best skills I've developed."

He said nothing, but looked into her face, searching.

"Perhaps I have gotten carried away," she said. "I apologize for monopolizing the conversation."

He shook his head. "I am bewildered." He smiled at her fondly. "Every time I think I have come to understand what it is that makes you remarkable, you open a new door. The first time I saw you, I noticed you were beautiful. And then you spoke, and I learned that you are funny. And then, you showed me that you are a woman of information. You are capable. You are kind," he said with a gentle smile, patting her letter on the table. "And now you show me that you are a philosopher."

He leaned across the small table until his face was very near her own. "I can only imagine," he whispered, "what amazing things you will open to my view in the coming days."

Her heart stuttered under his intense gaze. She reached for his hands. "I would hate to disappoint you," she said, smiling.

"I do not believe that is possible," he answered.

"You may have already seen everything impressive about me."

He laughed. "I doubt it. But that is a risk I am willing to take for as long as you will allow me to stand as a witness."

"I am not going anywhere," she said. "I promise."

❦

LAMENT

Words of love rise up the staircases
And travel the halls on the breeze.
No one will ever speak such words to me.

CHAPTER 14

The afternoon of the following day brought Lucas to the greenhouse as usual, but his step was quicker, his eyes even brighter than Hyacinth was used to seeing.

Without even a hello, Lucas began speaking. "You must have impressed Polly, for she sent a reply by return post." He held a folded paper out to her, his smile overspreading his whole face and threatening to split him in two.

Hyacinth took the proffered letter and placed it in her pocket.

"Will you not read it now?" he asked.

She wanted to turn the subject to ghosts and intruders, but when she saw his excitement, she smiled. "Are you so eager?" she asked.

"Indeed," he said. "Eager for you to get to know my sister."

Shaking her head, she said, "I shall be happy to do that at my leisure. For now, I should like to spend time with you."

It was as direct as she thought she could be. When he

agreed, she would open a new discussion about Rosa and the prowler.

He drew her to him and kissed her tenderly. "There," he murmured. He kissed her again. "And there," he said again. "That was indeed time well spent. Now read the letter."

His pure delight—and his warm kisses—overshadowed any frustration Hyacinth felt. She opened the letter, glanced over it, and began to read.

Dear Miss Bell,

What a kind and pleasant letter you have sent me. I am delighted to have a way to make friends with you. I accept your invitation to answer your three questions. Indeed, I believe I will be happy to comply with your wishes at all times.

There are many hopes in my heart. Sometimes they fight with the disappointments that threaten to suffocate them. Today, my pressing hope is that we find a way to meet. I hope that someday, I might have the pleasure of looking upon the face that my brother has become so fond of. Is that too bold? I pray you will forgive me if it is. I hope that your friendship with my brother continues to grow to the extent that I may take part in it.

You asked me to tell you about something I'm afraid of. In the world, there is much to fear, and I am not brave. Perhaps you know that I had a cousin, the child of our Aunt Carter. Rosa was my dearest friend. We grew up together and went to work together when we were grown. She became ill and died. I am sorry to tell you such sad news. Before she passed, I promised to remember her. That I would keep her always in my heart. I fear, Miss Bell, that despite my best attempts and efforts, I might forget her. That I will lose the sound of her singing or the image of her head tilting when she laughed. I know that you intended me to answer this question playfully, and I very much enjoyed your story of monkeys, but my great fear is not one that I can joke about. I strive to keep Rosa's spirit alive in my heart. Always. Sometimes I fear I cannot do it for much longer.

What makes me feel proud? There is nothing of which I am prouder than my dear brother, Lucas. He truly has the most wonderful heart. He works so hard. His every thought is for those he loves. And how, you might wonder, do I take pride in this, which is in no way an accomplishment of my own? The answer is that I give myself far too much credit for Lucas growing into the man he is. I cared for him as well as I could after our parents passed. Nothing pleased me as much in my life as helping him grow and learn. He has become a most remarkable man, and nothing I could ever do in my life will compare to helping him achieve his potential.

As I read the words I have just written, I see the strong difference between you and me. You are vibrant and accomplished and funny and clever. I am none of these, but I hope you will continue to write to me. Your temperament seems to combine all the things I wish I could be.

I enjoyed your letter so much, Miss Bell, and I hope that, even though I am not much like you, you can enjoy

*mine as well. If that is the case, I will wait impatiently
to hear from you again.*

    With sincerest warmth,

Polly Harding

Hyacinth looked up from the letter to see Lucas watching her. His expression spoke of his eagerness for the two women in his life to become friends.

She smiled at him and folded the letter. "Your sister has a warm heart."

His smile grew. "She does. I am glad her letter showed that heart to you."

"Would you like to read it?" she asked.

"Oh, I would not like to intrude," he said, but there was something in his look that belied his statement. If Hyacinth was any judge, Lucas wanted to read the letter very much.

"You do make an appearance in the message," she said, passing the letter across the table. "Perhaps you ought to know just how much your sister adores you."

He hesitated for only a moment before he reached for the paper.

She watched him read, fairly sure she knew which part of the letter softened his smile to a gentle look of humble gratitude. Her mind returned again and again to Polly's words about Rosa. Did the heartbroken ghost know that her cousin thought about her so faithfully? Hyacinth thought such knowledge could only bring Rosa peace.

Upon finishing, Lucas held the folded note to his heart for a moment before returning it to Hyacinth.

"Polly means so much to me. I would do anything to protect her."

The word surprised Hyacinth. "Protect her? From what?"

He mirrored her surprise. "From the world," he said. "There are dangers all around. People who want to hurt and wound and take the advantage."

"I suppose that is true," Hyacinth said. "But it is also true that there are delights all around, and people ready to share and accept and love."

He shook his head. "Those things are true for some. You, for instance. You are strong. You are vibrant and vital." His hands seemed to clench involuntarily. "Polly is not like you. She is ill, and the world is not kind to her."

Hyacinth did not know how to answer. What was he not telling her? What did he mean when he said Polly was ill? He had mentioned it before, but she assumed it meant only something simple. Was it more than a passing sickness she suffered at the season's change? Had she an impediment that made her journey through the world more difficult than Hyacinth's own? Than his?

She nodded, even though she did not understand. "*You* are kind to her, though, Lucas. And I shall be as well."

He held her eyes, and she felt his gratitude.

Now was the time. While he felt the glow of the sweet new friendship growing between Hyacinth and his sister, he was more likely to be forthcoming with stories of their cousin. "And what can you tell me of Rosa? She is Mrs. Carter's daughter and your sister's friend, and what else?"

He nodded. "She and Polly were nearly the same age. Friends as close as sisters. And so, by association, Rosa was like a sister to me as well. Rosa was more like you than Polly is. All my sister's gladness came from being home, staying inside, holding close to our routine. Rosa enjoyed a jest, an adventure, and an exploration."

Hyacinth loved every delicious detail. Lucas knew how to tell a good story after all. "Polly knew every bird by sight and by song. Rosa could set a trap for one and lure it into the house."

Hyacinth laughed at the image. "Her mother must have loved that."

Lucas's voice cradled his memory in tenderness. "My aunt would give anything to chase a bird from her kitchen one more time."

Hyacinth wondered at this. Only a few nights ago, the chicken in the kitchen had upset her more than Hyacinth might have imagined. Perhaps Mrs. Carter's distress was due to her grief, to a remembered event that would never recur, not because of any mess she had to repair.

Lucas continued. "The illness took us all by surprise. Her weakening was particularly difficult for Polly herself, who had always depended on Rosa's strength."

"That is a terrible trial. Poor Polly. Perhaps she found some new strength of her own," Hyacinth said, hoping it was true.

"I believe it is an ongoing struggle," Lucas answered. "Perhaps for all the rest of her life."

Hyacinth wanted to know why Rosa's ghost wandered the halls of Ashthorne. "Did Rosa have her mother with her? At the end? Did she receive ample medical care?"

Lucas watched her for a moment before replying. He

seemed to be considering how best to answer her question. "Her particular illness was something of a mystery to the physicians in London. Many of them urged Rosa to admit herself to a sanitorium. Some pressure was brought to bear. Several men of science and medicine were eager to watch the progression of her disease and tried to force her into an institution. An asylum."

Lucas looked at Hyacinth to see if his words shocked her. When she simply nodded, he went on. "But she wanted none of it, and Polly attended her through her last days."

Hyacinth had so many questions, and she wished Lucas was freer with information, for even her limited respect for social politeness prevented her from asking what would surely be taken as far too personal questions. What was this mysterious diagnosis? How quickly had Rosa's disease progressed? What had been her symptoms? Was Polly's illness the same as Rosa's had been? She did not wish to appear to be interrogating Lucas, but the scientist in her demanded information. Yet, she understood that what was far more important to Lucas than the medical mystery was the woman. His cousin. His sister's dearest friend.

Hyacinth would make notes of all her questions for later, and she would convey her sympathy to Mrs. Carter. Might the housekeeper be open to a conversation about her daughter's illness and death? Lucas's statement caused Hyacinth to wonder if the family was left with lingering questions that perhaps she could help answer. She remembered conversations with her own father, asking detailed questions about her mother's decline. Perhaps the housekeeper would not wish to speak of it, but if she did, Hyacinth might be of use to a woman who was, occasionally, kind to her. Perhaps her empathy might further open a door of friendship with Mrs. Carter.

When Lucas left for his own cottage that evening, Hyacinth wasted no time in saying good night to Mrs. Carter. She hoped the housekeeper would make her own way straight to bed so Hyacinth could wander wherever her whims took her.

After waiting a short interval, Hyacinth made her way back down to the kitchen, hoping to find a set of keys she could try in the doors leading off the servants' hidden hallway. Instead, she found Mrs. Carter in the kitchen, kneading dough on a floured board.

The woman must have heard her footsteps at the door, because she made a happy humming sound and said, "Good evening, dear," as she turned around to face Hyacinth.

The warm smile evaporated from her face like morning dew on a hot day. "Miss Bell," Mrs. Carter said in shock and surprise. "I did not expect you."

"Who did you think I was?" Hyacinth asked, knowing the words were wrong as soon as she said them. Presumptuous. Thoughtless. She had not earned the right to ask Mrs. Carter such a question.

The woman glared at Hyacinth, then schooled her features and said, "Mr. Harding, of course. Who else would be in the manor?"

It was clear Mrs. Carter did not require an answer.

Attempting to regain some of Mrs. Carter's occasional

warmth, Hyacinth asked, "Do you make all the bread yourself? I love the little brown loaves."

Mrs. Carter gave a single nod. "There is a satisfactory bakery in the village, but I prefer to do my own bread making when I have time."

"I've never made bread," Hyacinth said, as if Mrs. Carter had asked. "I'm told it takes a great deal of effort and many hours."

The housekeeper did not look up from her kneading. Hyacinth watched the tendons in her forearms as she pushed the mound of dough across the board. "Most worthwhile things require exertion and industry."

She glanced up for only a second, but it was long enough for Hyacinth to feel the rebuke. Did Mrs. Carter think Hyacinth's work with the orchids was not worthwhile? Did she consider Hyacinth lazy? Had she entered the hothouse and heard Hyacinth singing to the flowers? Or had she looked inside on an afternoon when she and Lucas had left the orchids and walked along the shore?

Might she make an unfavorable report to Mr. Whitbeck?

Hyacinth's stomach knotted with new worry. As Mrs. Carter had not invited her to sit, she made an awkward wave, said good night, and left the kitchen.

At least Mrs. Carter would be busy in the kitchen a while. Perhaps quite a long while.

Hyacinth crept up the staircase leading to the forbidden wing, lifting her feet as if she could prevent her steps making any sound.

She walked directly to the end of the hallway. "Rosa?"

she called, her voice as quiet as she could make it and still be heard through the door.

Hyacinth heard nothing.

She felt confident Rosa would answer eventually, so she continued to call.

Nothing.

No light shone beneath the door, and not a sound carried back to her, not even a breath of the usual wind.

The silence felt more frightening and oppressive than all the wailing and crying she'd heard every night she'd lived here. Why wasn't Rosa answering? Something was wrong. She tasted fear at the back of her throat.

No matter that she did not know what she feared. No matter that nothing in this house, including a ghost, had hurt her. An inexpressible terror pressed against her heart. With a shiver of dread, she ran the length of the hall and down the stairs and back up the other side. She did not stop until she'd locked herself in her bedroom.

She lit a lamp and placed it on the table beside her bed.

"Eleanor," she said, her voice shaking. "I feel so foolish. I must be the only woman in the world to find herself scared out of her wits by *not* hearing a ghost."

LAMENT

These halls are like a prison.
I must get out, feel the air surround me.
I long to hear birdsong and walk among trees.
I am confined to this house,
But who imprisons me?
Is it only myself?

CHAPTER 15

By morning, Hyacinth's fears had washed away with the rain. Several hours in the hothouse and even the chill of autumn rain burned away. For her midday meal, she took her second apple and one of Mrs. Carter's small brown loaves and stood in the hothouse doorway, out of the rain but feeling the fresh breeze. Looking out toward the formal garden, she felt grateful her work required her to be inside.

A nearby twig snapped at someone's footstep, and Hyacinth looked up, a ready smile on her face to greet Lucas.

But it was not Lucas.

James, Mr. Gardner's assistant, stepped close to the hothouse door with a leer on his face.

"What are you doing here?" Hyacinth asked, her shock at seeing the man apparent in her voice.

James tugged at the tail of his threadbare coat and scoffed. His odor of stale drink and unwashed body and strong tobacco assaulted her. "Not very welcoming. Aren't you going to invite me inside?"

She had no intention of doing so, but it was easier to ask another question than to say no outright.

"Did Mr. Gardner send you?" she asked, attempting a slightly more gracious tone.

He grunted, which was not an answer at all. He walked closer to the doorway, and she stepped back inside the hothouse. He immediately took advantage of her movement, coming another step nearer.

Hyacinth planted her feet. He would not intimidate her. Not even when he leaned in the open doorway, bringing his sour smells with him.

"What is it you need, sir?" She would not use his given name. Familiarity would weaken her against him.

He sneered at her. "Just information. Need to know about the sick girl."

Hyacinth's mouth dropped open. She wasn't sure what she'd expected James to say, but it was certainly not that.

Her confusion spilled out in a flood of speech. "There is no sick girl here. The family is not on the property, as you know. There are no children at the manor at all."

Hyacinth felt more baffled than ever. Why would an assistant in a garden shop need information about a sick child in a family who was half a world away?

He shook his head. "Not children. Just want to find the girl."

His clarification was no help at all. Was he drunk? It would go far in explaining his wretched smell.

He straightened, and his next words came out differently. Uniform. Unnatural. Forced. "The company is interested in her condition."

The statement sounded like something he'd been instructed to say, but she couldn't make any sense of it. Though even if she knew exactly what he was after, she wouldn't give it to him.

She tried for an air of superiority, a voice of earned contempt. "As you can see, there is no one here but me, and I cannot help you. If you have questions regarding the manor, you may call at the door for Mrs. Carter."

The man turned and spat on the ground, rainwater running down his hair. With a snarl, he cursed. "She's no help at all. You want a thing, you got to find a way to take the thing."

Thing? What did he want to take from Mrs. Carter? And how could it possibly relate to a sick girl? Thoughts of Rosa flooded her mind, and Hyacinth's skin crawled. Was he interested in Rosa's story? His anger at Mrs. Carter would make a dreadful sort of sense if he'd wanted information about Rosa's illness and Mrs. Carter had refused to give it to him.

So now he—what?—wandered the manor looking for her ghost? Asking about her "condition"?

The very idea was preposterous, but Hyacinth had seen enough of the unbelievable in the past week to know she could not dismiss it out of hand.

At least Rosa was safe. This man couldn't hurt someone who had already passed away.

"There is nothing on the estate that is of any concern to you," Hyacinth said, but her bravado was beginning to crack. Everything about this man was horrible, and she needed him gone. Away from her. Out of the hothouse doorway. Off Ashthorne's land.

James made a feral, growling sound in his throat.

Hyacinth's knees trembled in fear.

"The caretaker is patrolling the grounds," she said. Though she had no idea if it was true, she tried to sound believable. "He has been here longer than I have and will understand your concern better. Perhaps you will see him on your way off the property."

She moved to close the door between them, but James pressed it open with his forearm. She was certain he knew his height advantage was intimidating.

Not to mention his stench.

Hyacinth felt bile rise in her throat as he leaned deeper inside the hothouse.

"I think you understand me fine, flower girl."

She shook her head. No. She did not understand. Not in the slightest.

She knew her fear lay clear on her face, in every trembling muscle, behind her eyes. With heroic effort, she clenched her jaw and matched his lean.

She needed the bearing of her older sister now. Pitching her voice low and deep and imagining dismissing a bothersome pest, she said, "You may go now."

Her comment must have surprised him as much as it did her, because he turned and walked away, muttering and cursing as he splashed along the muddy path.

Did the hothouse have a lock? Could she bar the door against another intrusion?

Hyacinth's stomach roiled, and she dropped the halfeaten apple onto the floor. She had no appetite to finish her lunch. Would she ever want to eat again? Her fear mixed with the lingering odor of the man hung about her, clinging to the inside of her nose and throat, threatening to gag her.

She wanted Lucas, and immediately. How often had he simply appeared in the hothouse at nothing but a wish? Now that her longing was more desperate, he was elsewhere.

If she called for Lucas, James might hear, and she did not want to give that horrible man any reason to reappear. If she attempted to cross the manor's property, would she run into James before she found Lucas? Right now, she dared not attempt it.

And if Lucas did come, what would she say to him? What did any of this mean? How could she understand anything when it was all such nonsense? A sick girl? The company? Hyacinth truly hated the way fear muddled her mind and clouded her thinking. She resented her own weakness and despised the man for his intrusion.

But resentment was no use to her now. She could not simply stand at the glass wall of the hothouse and wait for Lucas to pass by and notice her distress. She slipped out of the orchid house and turned along the path opposite from the one James had taken.

The rain had eased to a chill drizzle that seemed to hang in the air and collect on her skin. Passing the rose garden with its unused fountain, she glanced around for Lucas. She could see no one. She thought about searching the sculpture garden for him, but a flicker of white caught her eye.

In the trees, a figure in a gauzy dress moved quietly parallel with the path.

"Rosa?" Hyacinth called.

The ghost did not stop, and Hyacinth followed her as

she picked up speed and darted deeper into the woods. Rain fell, as it seemed always to do, and thunder rolled across the estate.

"Rosa, wait, please."

She must ask her if she'd seen the man. She would know if James was the nighttime prowler. If he was, then he could get inside Ashthorne Hall. Hyacinth shuddered at the thought of him in her room.

If Rosa heard her call, she did not stop. She did not even turn.

Fine. Rosa could ignore her, but Hyacinth would follow.

Hyacinth kept her distance and maintained the same speed as the ghost, jumping over brambles and grateful at every step that she was still in her working skirts rather than a typical day dress with all its yards and yards of decorative fabric. Branches pulled at her arms, tangling and tugging at her thick braid.

Rosa seemed to glide easily through the wood, dodging a fallen limb and leaping over a bush that nearly tripped Hyacinth.

Picking up speed, Hyacinth drew closer, seeing that Rosa held her arms out, reaching for something. What was she running toward? Or what from? Had she seen James? Had he seen her, threatened her? Hyacinth felt a need to know, to help, for even though Rosa had not spoken last night, would not answer her now, the ghost was, in a strange and wonderful way, her friend.

Hyacinth crashed into a low branch, made invisible by cloud and shadow. She stumbled to the ground, cracking her shins against the branch. She came to her knees and back to her feet, climbing over the obstruction.

Mere steps forward and she was out of the woods, a break in the trees leading to a small cottage surrounded by yew hedges and a clipped lawn. Had Rosa entered the cottage? Could she do so as easily as she seemed to enter Hyacinth's bedroom in the night? Hyacinth could see no sign of Rosa, no flutters of white, no movement around the property.

She made for the door and raised her hand to pound upon it, calling out, "Hello?"

Before she could make contact, the door opened, and Lucas stepped out, backlit by a warm glow of candlelight in the room.

Hyacinth gasped. "It's you," she said, her arm still raised.

"Hello," he answered, smiling and pulling the door closed behind him. "This is a lovely surprise."

His calm response was so unexpected she could do nothing but stand before him, perplexed and gulping air.

He leaned his back against the closed door, standing with Hyacinth in the drizzling rain. Her lungs seared from her unplanned activity, and in her confusion, she did not know which startling story to tell first: James or Rosa?

A moment's thought was enough to decide.

"Someone is on the estate," she said, her breath catching and her words ragged and shaky.

He tilted his head close to hers and smiled. "Do you mean besides us?"

She was in no humor for his flirting. "Yes." She decided to start with the easiest explanation. "You asked me to keep an eye out for a prowler."

Lucas looked surprised and a bit amused. "I don't believe I said any such thing."

She shook her head. "You said someone has been seen here, walking on the property, who does not belong. A man on the cliff."

With a nod, he said, "Ah. Right. Though how you went from wandering stranger to something as menacing as prowler, I have no idea." He smiled again, all his warmth and love right there on his face.

Though she wanted to sink into the warmth of his arms, she said, "I saw him. Spoke to him. I know him."

"You know him?" Lucas repeated. "From London?"

Hyacinth shook her head. "What? No, from Mr. Gardner's greenhouse."

Lucas whispered a word Hyacinth was sure he did not want her to hear.

She continued. "I worry he's mad. He made no sense at all—speaking of girls and illness and companies and conditions."

Lucas made an effort to appear casual, but she read deep concern in his eyes. "I see. And where did you see him?"

"In the orchid house. He tried to come inside, but I stopped him."

The words came out easily, but the memory of her fear covered her like wet wool, suffocating and rank.

"I'll take a look. See if he's still about the place. If he is, I'll warn him off, and you'll never be bothered by him again."

With that, Lucas jogged away, leaving Hyacinth standing in front of his cottage door in the rain.

Alone.

Naturally he could not invite her inside his house. But must she go away? Hyacinth wanted to look inside, peer into a window, see if Rosa had entered Lucas's cottage. If Hyacinth asked directly, would he insist the ghost was not there?

She felt no guilt at opening Ashthorne's locked bedroom doors, but she would not invade Lucas's privacy by stepping uninvited into his home. She walked toward the looming walls of the manor.

Looking back over her shoulder, craning her neck to study the grassy clearing around the cottage, Hyacinth saw nothing but the little house, silvered by raindrops, warm candlelight glowing at a window.

No intruder. No man running through the trees. No ghost.

She turned back toward Ashthorne Hall, head low against the increasing rain.

Something fluttered at the corner of her vision, white against green. Something at the edge of the path near the tallest trees. Hyacinth moved to examine it. Hanging there, snagged on a bramble, was a piece of white cloth. Hyacinth untangled it gently from the thorns.

She folded the white fabric and tucked it into her sleeve. She would make a careful study of it once she was back in the house.

She saw no sign of Lucas, James, Rosa, or Mrs. Carter as she made her way into the house and upstairs to her room. Mostly she was glad to be alone, but she still wondered why Rosa had fled instead of speaking with her.

Before entering her room, she looked over her shoulder, back down the hall, unsure whether she more feared or hoped to see something glowing there, far along the north hallway. If Rosa was there, she was evading her. If she was not, how far might the ghost girl flee to avoid the man James? Would she leave Ashthorne altogether? Hyacinth hoped not. She had grown fond of the ghost's company.

Hyacinth lit the taper in its holder beside her bed, and then she lit several more, giving the corner of the room a warm glow. She sat in the chair and pulled the white cloth from the woods out of her sleeve. There was a small snag where it had pulled against the brambles. The edges were seamed, not ripped, so the fabric was not torn from something else. It was roughly a square, perhaps ten inches along each side. Two thin ribbons attached to the top made it look like an apron for a tiny child or a large doll.

The cloth itself, thin and gauzy, was soft, probably from many washings. A handkerchief? If so, what were the ribbons for? Hyacinth turned it again and again in her hands, looking for clues as to what purpose it might serve. She held it up to her face and realized it was the perfect size for a veil.

A fluttering, white face covering.

Much like she had seen over the face of Rosa's ghost.

Hyacinth held the veil up to her face, bringing the top of the fabric to her forehead and tying the ribbons at the back of her hair. She could see through the cloth, but as she looked into the mirror, she saw how obscured her features were.

Did this veil belong to Rosa? Was it, perhaps, the veil that covered her face for burial? As soon as the thought entered her mind, Hyacinth ripped the fabric from her own face and threw it to the floor. A violent shudder shook her.

She took a moment to collect herself. The cloth was

clean. There was not a mar on it aside from the snag she had made pulling it from the brambles. Admittedly, she had few experiences with the grave dressings of ghosts, but her brain told her thudding heart there was nothing otherworldly about this veil.

She picked it up from the floor and, with still-trembling fingers, made a final inspection. The language and practices of scientific discovery helped calm her further. Taking the filmy veil in her fingers, she inspected the stitching.

There, in the lower corner, sewn in white thread on the white cloth, a tiny five-petal flower and the letters RC.

Rosa Carter.

‍❦

LAMENT

I cannot continue to pretend.
I will not lie anymore.
She has been honest with me, and I must do the same,
Whatever the consequence.
I never knew how much the idea of honesty could hurt.

CHAPTER 16

Listening at her bedroom door, she heard only the ever-present whistling of the wind through Ashthorne's hallways. Without lamp or candle that might call attention to herself, she eased the door open and walked silently into the hall. One step after another took her to the landing, and she moved steadily down the south staircase and back up the north, straining her eyes at what looked like a light near the end of the hall.

As she moved closer, she was no longer in any doubt. A line of light shone from beneath a closed door at the end of the hall.

Rosa?

Hyacinth approached, ready to call out, but stopped short when she heard Lucas's voice.

"You can't speak to her either. It's not safe."

A raspy, crackling laugh followed. "Do you think I'm going to hurt her? I would never, even if I had the strength."

Lucas made a sound of exasperation. "I meant it isn't safe for *you*."

"She will not hurt me. Besides, I spend all my time locked inside this room. How much danger could I be in?"

Hyacinth was startled to find that she was close to laughter. Her ghost was witty.

Now Lucas sighed. "Will you please trust me? Stay hidden. Do not wander inside the manor. Or out. And please, do not speak to her. I wouldn't ask it if it wasn't important. I only want to protect you." His voice became quiet, and Hyacinth leaned toward the door to hear better. "There's so little I can do for you now."

The dear man. He wanted Hyacinth to stay away from his cousin's ghost. For protection. What bizarre idea must he hold about post-mortal relationships if he imagined Hyacinth a threat to Rosa's spirit?

She did not hear Rosa's reply, but she was sure Lucas would walk out of the room at any moment. It would never do for him to find her here. She considered running back to her room, but as the architecture of the hallway required her to go down and back up the stairs to get there, he surely would see her on the staircase. Almost without thinking, she pulled a pin from her hair and unlocked the room next door, entered, and silently closed the door behind her.

Her practice had made her adept, and even in her anxious state, she grinned to herself in the dark.

Falling to her knees behind the closed door, she lifted her eye to the keyhole and stared at the thin line of light that painted the carpeted hall. Would Lucas leave the room? At this strange angle, would she be able to tell? Would there be enough light for her to see anything at all?

Only a moment later, the light spilled into the hall in a

wide swath, radiating outward from the now-open door. The light did not remain long. With a return to near-darkness, she heard the lock click, heard Lucas release a sigh. Then she saw the shape of him as he moved past the door where she knelt.

Forcing herself to wait, she counted to thirty. Was it long enough? Would Lucas be out of the hallway and down the stairs?

She counted to thirty again for good measure, then crept out of the room and tapped her finger against the next door. The line of light still shone at her feet.

"Rosa?" she whispered. "Will you please speak to me?"

What she heard in reply was not the wail of haunting but more like mortal sniffling and sobbing. Was this the ghost who had laughed at Lucas only moments ago?

"Rosa?" she whispered again. "Will you let me help you?"

The light shifted beneath the door, and Hyacinth wondered at the ability of a ghost to cast a shadow. How much more impossible was this than anything else she'd witnessed in this hallway?

"Please," she said, her palm spread on the door as if to support the being on the other side. "May I come inside?"

This time an answering whisper came through the door. "I wish it was possible."

Heartened, Hyacinth again pulled a pin from her hair. "It is. I can unlock the door."

"You misunderstand," the voice said. "I have a key. All the keys. But I cannot defy my brother's wish."

Brother?

She'd never heard of Rosa having a brother, had she? Did Mrs. Carter have another child?

Or did Hyacinth misunderstand yet again?

Hyacinth stopped, one hand on the door and the other holding a hairpin. In one of those familiar moments of rapid revelation, she felt her mind swirl, spinning out all that she thought she understood for closer examination.

"Your brother?" she repeated.

Rosa did not have a brother. Polly did.

This misinformation was harder to dislodge than any she'd yet tried. After a few moments of grasping and considering, Hyacinth began to piece together a new explanation.

Lucas told her his sister wanted to write to Hyacinth. So she wrote a letter which he delivered.

He told her Polly was in London.

No, she reminded herself. Lucas told her Polly was *outside* London. Cornwall was outside London. Technically true.

It was not true enough. He hid the fact that Polly was here, in Ashthorne, with them.

He may not have lied outright, but he had deceived her. He was still deceiving her.

With a physical effort, Hyacinth shook her mind free of what she had once been sure was the truth, making room for new information.

"Polly?" she asked. "Is it you?"

In answer, the girl behind the door gave a shuddering breath and a humming of assent.

"What about Rosa?" Hyacinth wanted to ask more, to discover if all she had assumed about the ghost for the past few days was another misunderstanding.

"Rosa died." The two simple words in that rasping whisper nearly broke Hyacinth's heart.

She wanted to ask about Rosa's ghost, to discover if the halls of Ashthorne were indeed haunted, but was sure this— whispering through the door in the dark of night—wasn't the way.

"But you are well." It wasn't a question, but Hyacinth was not sure it was a true statement either. Was there something in between?

"I am ill, but I am surviving."

Hyacinth put her forehead to the door. "Polly, will you let me in? Please, so we can speak properly?"

Another pause. "I will frighten you."

Hyacinth would never laugh at the girl, but she was certain Polly would not scare her.

"I believe I can be brave," she answered.

Polly was quiet for so long Hyacinth wondered if she had decided against speaking to her again.

Then a key scraped the lock and the knob turned. Hyacinth wanted to push through the door and take Polly into her arms in a hug, but she resisted. Even through the closed door, Hyacinth could hear Polly's voice was full of emotions, and one of those feelings was undoubtedly fear.

Hyacinth would give her nothing more to be afraid of.

The door opened slowly, but only when Hyacinth was all the way in the room could she see the other woman.

As before, Polly wore a fluttering white dress, her face covered with a gauzy veil exactly like the one Hyacinth had found in the woods. Now, though, standing close in a room glowing with lamplight, Hyacinth noticed what she had not seen clearly in her stolen glances.

This was not a specter, floating and glowing and gliding through the halls. This was a woman as alive as herself.

Hands behind her back, clutching the doorknob, Polly Harding pressed herself into the door, giving Hyacinth as much space as the room allowed.

Hyacinth took a step forward.

Releasing the doorknob, Polly raised a hand and then lowered it. She repeated the movement twice again before her fingers touched the hem of the veil over her face. With an audible exhale, she removed the veil, and Hyacinth saw Polly's face.

She did not speak. Could not move. Almost dared not breathe. The shock of seeing Polly so closely nearly turned Hyacinth to stone.

The damage was difficult to take in. Shocking. Dreadful. Only in photographs and illustrations accompanying newspaper articles about necrosis had Hyacinth seen anything like Polly's ravaged cheek, her sunken jaw. No drawing could communicate the devastation of seeing such damage in person. No photograph, however detailed, could show every angle and element of the wreck of this face. A picture on paper did not live and breathe like the woman standing in front of her did.

Hyacinth wondered at the pain Polly must be feeling— must always feel. How was this woman even standing, let alone running through the hallways and grounds, gliding as if her feet barely touched the floors? She gazed at Polly's cheek. Near the jaw, through puckered skin, bone decay was evident. How could such trauma not cause tremendous pain?

Hyacinth's scientific mind allowed her to categorize and

note the obvious damage to Polly's face. Beneath her right eye rose a bulbous swelling. The jawbone on the left appeared to be disintegrating, causing an imbalanced appearance that looked excruciating and tender.

When Polly opened her mouth to speak, Hyacinth saw a slight glow emanating from her gums. It made her face shine with a ghastly, poisonous light.

"Hello, Hyacinth."

No wonder she had assumed this was the face of a ghost.

Hyacinth felt grateful for her scientific training. Who might have guessed that years of making observations might lessen the horror of this first impression? As she stood only steps away from Polly, she knew what was important now.

Not crying out. Not mentioning the sores, the swellings. Not asking about the damage. Polly's ravaged face only mattered in that it was Polly's.

Hyacinth held out a hand, palm up. "I am so delighted to meet you," she said.

Several long seconds passed before Polly lifted her hand and touched Hyacinth's fingers with her own. For a moment, they stood facing each other, fingertips touching, searching each other's eyes.

"I'm sorry to be such a fright," Polly said. She pointed at herself, gesturing to the general area of her chin. "It's called phossy jaw."

Hyacinth wanted to deny being afraid, but there was no way to ignore her unwitting reaction to seeing Polly. She knew what she was witnessing, for newspapers had been reporting instances of "phossy jaw" for several years.

But knowing and seeing landed in very distinct sections

of Hyacinth's brain. She gave herself a moment to formulate a true and honest response that was also thoughtful and kind.

She held Polly's hand more firmly in her own and said, "And I apologize for assuming I knew what I was seeing and hearing. I hope my calling you by Rosa's name did not make your sadness worse."

Polly shook her head. "We do not often speak her name aloud anymore. It was good to hear it from you."

Hyacinth could only imagine the ache behind Polly's words. She thought of their brief, whispered conversations. Had Polly ever actually told Hyacinth she was Rosa? She thought not. Hyacinth had assumed, and Polly had not corrected her. There had been misunderstandings, but not lies.

As her shock lessened, she felt her face relax into a smile. "Polly, I am delighted that you and I are both here at Ashthorne and we can finally meet. I do hope we can be friends."

She knew she was talking too much and wondered if she ought to give Polly a bit more space.

"Friends. Yes. I like that idea very much." Polly wrapped her fingers more and more tightly around Hyacinth's own and smiled. Her ruined face took on an impossibly painful beauty.

"Can we sit?" Polly asked. "I am rather tired."

She gestured to a pair of chairs set beside the bedroom's screened fireplace. Hyacinth nodded and followed her, taking a seat.

Hyacinth wanted to ask so many questions, wished to have her curiosity satisfied on every count. But she also knew that Polly was not well and would not want to be interrogated. She would let Polly lead their conversation.

"I suppose Lucas explained about me," she said, and Hyacinth felt a wave of sadness. As though a person could be "explained" by the diagnosis of an illness. There was so much more to Polly than her deformity, than her pain, than her fear.

"He told me that you contracted an illness from your work in London. He did not say what it was—either the work or the illness. But before he told me that, he told me much more. For instance," she continued, a grin spreading across her face, "he told me you never once let him win when you were playing tag or marbles as children."

Polly's answering laugh was gentle and ringing, like the soft sound of a bell. "That may be true, but he would cry when he lost, so I let him have all the best marbles."

Hyacinth waited to see if Polly would speak again about the distant past or if she would offer information from her more recent history.

The young woman looked at her hands and then back at Hyacinth.

"When I followed Rosa to London, I had some money, but not enough to live comfortably for long. I could have saved money by staying and working in Suttonsbury, but I loved the idea of leading a completely different kind of life.

"The match factory hired mostly women, because our fingers were more delicate, or that's what they told us. Compared to the other girls we worked with, Rosa and I had very comfortable lives and lodgings. Many of the factory girls were from impoverished circumstances and lived six or more to a room. Rosa and I might have come home at any time, but we came to the city with a bit of money, and we were having an adventure. We were the lucky ones there.

"We did our work. We collected our pay. We spent most of it again on board and food and clothing and entertainment. A play one week, a museum the next. Having work was in some ways a necessity and in others, a lark."

Hyacinth did not reply, but she nodded to show Polly she was listening.

"It may be hard for you to believe, but I was strong then. Strong enough to stand hours every day in a factory, dipping matches in phosphorus, cutting sticks, and placing finished matches in boxes. When I think about it now, the whole experience seems impossible. How could it have seemed so simple to stand for so many hours, working alongside the others? Now I find myself exhausted by a walk over the path to Lucas's cottage or a trip to the music room and back up the stairs. And how could I not realize the poisonous fumes of the chemicals were eating at my teeth and jaws? But I didn't know. None of us understood what was happening right before our eyes."

She tugged at the sleeves of her dress and went on.

"Rosa and I loved being in the city, surrounded by new experiences and all those people. When Rosa fell ill, all the excitement drained away. I went to work, and then I came home and cared for Rosa. I watched the progression of her disease. I shared in her worry when her teeth began to fall out. I felt her horror at catching her reflection in a mirror. I heard her struggle for breath when a coughing fit gripped her. By the time she began experiencing seizures, she no longer worried about the swellings and the oddness of her appearance. You might think letting go of her worries was a good sign, but no. It was most horrible to see her drift into indifference. When she no longer cared, she no longer fought to live."

Polly touched a knuckle to the corner of her eye, as if to stop a tear before it fell. "Then the symptoms began in me. First a toothache. There were rules—no complaints. If a match girl told the bosses her tooth hurt, she was instructed to get it removed. Any further complaints and the girl would be sacked. I suffered in silence. I did not want Rosa to see my pain, and I did not want to lose the work I could still do. Then came the muscle pain. Headaches. Stomach complaints. I stopped going to work; I had no choice. I sat by Rosa's side, watching strength drain from her body and her spirit, knowing it would be my turn soon."

With a glance at Hyacinth, Polly asked, "Does it hurt you to hear this?"

Reaching across the space between them, Hyacinth took hold of Polly's hand. "I am honored to be trusted with your story."

With Polly's next blink, a tear rolled down her ravaged cheek.

"The company sent doctors to our home to examine Rosa. They wanted her to go into a sanitorium, somewhere they could watch her illness progress. She refused to spend the end of her life under examination, so she told them to go."

Hyacinth wondered how the doctors reacted to a dismissal from a sick young woman. If the company wanted to watch the progress of Rosa's disease, they must have resented anything getting in the way. And they must have understood the illness stemmed from the working conditions in the factory.

Polly continued her story. "When Rosa's time was short, I wrote to Aunt Ellen, telling her she should come. But the end came faster than I thought it would. I held Rosa's hand as she died."

Polly's voice was firm, but tears streamed down her face. "I hope Aunt Ellen can forgive me someday for not sending word to her sooner."

Hyacinth wanted to comfort Polly, but nothing she could say would take away her pain. The two sat together in silence.

With a shuddering breath, Polly looked into Hyacinth's eyes. "I have seen my death, and it is devastating. But it is not yet upon me. I want to live while I can."

Through a lump in her throat, Hyacinth whispered, "I want that for you as well."

Polly's smile was enough to break Hyacinth's heart. She understood every word Lucas had said about wanting to protect his sister. It was also Hyacinth's wish now.

And in the same instant, she understood the threat the man James made in the hothouse. The sick girl. The company's interest in her condition. For reasons she could not fathom, the matchstick factory owners and doctors wanted to watch Polly like they wanted to watch Rosa. And they were willing to send someone to menace her into compliance.

Hyacinth vowed within herself that she would prevent James from coming anywhere near Polly. If she had to bar every door herself and stand guard, she would keep him out.

Barred doors. Scraped locking mechanisms. Was James

the one who had tossed the furniture in that locked bedroom? Had he left the note warning the reader of it to avoid speaking?

Hyacinth vowed that, beginning now, she would stop making quick assumptions. She would be diligent in questioning her conclusions and checking and double-checking her inferences. Test everything. Assume nothing.

Hyacinth realized she and Polly had been sitting in silence for some time. "Thank you for helping me understand you," she said. "I appreciate your trust in me."

"And thank you for listening," Polly said. "I grow so tired of this illness, and yet it is always on my mind."

She squeezed Polly's hands again. "If it is agreeable to you, I propose we only discuss your health when you wish it and when I can be helpful to you. Otherwise, I think we can both agree that *you* are more interesting than any illness."

Another trickle of tears fell from Polly's eyes as she took in Hyacinth's remark. She whispered, "You cannot possibly understand what that means to me. It seems like forever since I felt like any other part of my life held any interest at all."

Hyacinth hoped she would be strong enough to support Polly when she needed her, but she was certain she could easily and regularly discuss nonmedical interests. She only hoped Polly would not grow tired of hearing about orchids.

Orchids. As soon as she had the thought, a ripple of fear ran over her shoulders. So much had happened since she had stepped away from the orchids that afternoon.

She needed to look in on the hothouse.

❦

LAMENT

Oh, to have a friend again.
The feeling is sweet and surprising.
But she must leave me, too.
This is my life.
Everyone leaves, and
I am destined to be alone.

CHAPTER 17

Night fell within a cloak of mist. A chill breeze from the
sea blew across the estate. Branches swayed in the wind like
elderly women fanning themselves in hot ballrooms. Every
step from the kitchen door to the hothouse felt heavy, like a
menace lurked and threatened to pull Hyacinth under each
stone in the path.

She wished she was not walking the path alone. This was
always a more pleasant walk when she was with Lucas.

What was Lucas doing now? After he had left Polly's
room, after he told her not to speak with Hyacinth, where
did he go?

And why did it matter to him that Polly not communicate with Hyacinth except by letter? Did he need to know
each word they shared? Even though he had encouraged their
correspondence, did he not truly want them to be friends?
Did he have something to fear if they grew close without
him?

Lucas wanted to keep Polly, his beloved sister, the person he loved most, from knowing her. Hearing him tell Polly

that Hyacinth was a danger to her was a terrible blow. She thought he trusted her, thought he loved her. She dared to hope he might grow to love her more every day. Every year, forever. Had she misunderstood everything? She had been so wrong about so many things lately, might she have misread Lucas as well? Had he played her false all along?

She had been at Ashthorne mere days, and in those days, she had grown to love this man. And in return, he gave her kisses and kept his secrets.

What might he say once he knew she and Polly had talked this evening? Once, only a day ago, perhaps only hours ago, Hyacinth was certain Lucas loved her. In the very short span of their acquaintance, she was sure he thought only of her. But when he spoke about her to his sister, it was with warnings and prohibitions. What would he think of her now?

Hyacinth entered the orchid house and instantly forgot all her selfish troubles in the space of a breath.

Disaster.

Within the hot, humid walls of the glass enclosure, every pot, every plant, every rooting tray lay tossed and tumbled, thrown from their places. Hanging varieties of orchids were knocked to the ground. Specimens that had been growing for decades lay overturned and smashed. Even some of the smaller tables were tipped over onto their sides. Mosses were torn from their stones. Blooms and blossoms lay scattered, plants knocked about with roots in the air, others crushed by bootheels. Hyacinth felt each plant must be gasping as much as she was herself.

Mr. Whitbeck's prized orchids, the remarkable plants he had collected over three decades, those he'd crossbred himself, the flowers that gave a touch of summertime elegance to each room of the manor house, all lay on their sides, stems bent, blooms ripped away, roots snapped off. On every table, Hyacinth discovered new measures of destruction.

She stood in the center of the hothouse for several long minutes, slowly turning from table to table, taking in the disaster before her. Cracked window glass, broken pots, and potting compounds were strewn across the floor.

"Oh, my poor darlings. I am so sorry."

Hyacinth had often been teased by her father for treating the orchids in her care as if they had human emotions and re-action. She laughed along with him, but secretly she knew it was true. After all the love she poured into their care, she was confident they returned that love, that she and the flowers breathed the same air.

She had no doubt the orchids felt tonight's attack. The damage went beyond root structure and bud formation and into the heart of each plant. She knelt on the floor and gath-ered stems and leaves, blossoms and buds into her hands, keening as she lifted them to the nearest table.

Almost no plant was left untouched, but few were ruined beyond hope of repair. It appeared as if the orchids had been tossed in a fit of temper as opposed to an orderly attack in-tended to cause lasting damage.

Vandalism.

Punishment. And if that was the attempt, it was success-ful, for certainly this was painfully punishing.

Who could do such a thing? And why? Was this the way James retaliated for her resistance and defiance earlier in the day? Was he still on the property? Still inside the hothouse?

She spun around, looking across the expanse of Mr. Whitbeck's ruined treasure, but saw no one. Holding her breath, she listened for any sound of movement or breathing. Nothing. She was quite sure she was alone.

She knew that as long as she remained in the hothouse, there was no way to know for certain why the destruction had taken place. Her questions would have to wait for answers.

Questions or no, answers or no, she had work to do.

She stood and removed her notebook from her pocket. Moving around and through the hothouse in an orderly manner, she stopped at each orchid plant, flipping through her notes to see if she could reliably identify the least damaged ones. When she found plants she was certain she recognized, she marked the original drawing, relocated the surviving plant to its original space in the hothouse, and drew a new sketch, marking leaf damage, loss of bloom, number of swellings, spars, and buds. She hardly knew how much time passed, so devoted was she to reporting as accurately as possible the state of each orchid.

How long, she wondered, would it take for a message to reach Mr. Whitbeck in India? And how long must she wait for a response? Would he blame her for this dreadful damage?

It would be unfair to assign her the fault, and at the same time, she would understand completely. She blamed herself, after all. She was not responsible for the destruction of the hothouse, but she was responsible for the flowers.

As she moved from plant to plant, replacing them in their established spots on the tables, she told them they were strong survivors.

She hummed and sang comforting songs, and if anyone

had asked, she might have said the songs were for the orchids. In fact, Hyacinth stood in great need of comfort herself, and she had learned years ago that she must not wait for someone else to come to her aid. The world was full of grief, and the best way out of it was through. Often, the only way through was alone.

LAMENT

I never knew that danger
Was a feeling,
Like cold wind
Or hot sun
Or suffocating humidity.
But now I feel it
In the house, in the walls.
Always around me.

CHAPTER 18

Long into the dark night, Hyacinth bent over what re-mained of Mr. Whitbeck's treasured collection, replanting where possible, attaching new stakes, and recovering any still-serviceable pots.

Body aching, she vowed to keep working until every plant was attended to. The pile of unrecoverable stems grew taller by the hour, but Hyacinth knew her responsibility.

Even if Mr. Whitbeck sent her away, she wanted to save as much of his orchid garden as she could.

Her eyes stung, longing to close, and her head grew heavy. The songs she sang to the flowers became nonsense, and even when she tried to stop herself, the words continued to tumble from her in waterfalls of gibberish.

By the time her exhaustion reached the point where she was likely to do more damage to the orchids than good, Hyacinth made her way out of the hothouse. Looking over her shoulder at what remained of the mess, a brief vision of the orchids' former glory overtook her. She would work day and night to get the collection back to its state of perfection.

Day and night for as long as it took, but she could do no more just now.

Steps heavy and slow, Hyacinth wondered if Mr. Isaac Newton had studied the effects of extreme fatigue on gravitational pull. She'd have liked to have a word with him.

A few more steps to the kitchen. Then down the hall and across the entryway, then up the stairs, along the deserted south hallway, and into bed. She could not imagine walking up the north steps to tell Polly what had happened in the hothouse. Another day. After a rest.

As she reached for the kitchen door, Hyacinth sighed in relief. So very close to sleep and sweet, dreamy oblivion. She turned the knob, but the door stuck beneath her hand. She rattled the handle, but the door would not open.

Locked? Why?

In all the times she'd come through this door, it had never been locked before. She did not wish to wake Mrs. Carter, but neither did she wish to stay outside all night. The wind blew cold, and she had no patience left for pretended politeness. She had no energy to shout, but she pounded on the door, cracking her fist against the wood.

There were only seconds of silence, then she heard shuffling.

"Who is there?" a voice rasped.

What a relief to hear that voice. "Polly?" Hyacinth said on a sigh. "It's me."

The sound of key releasing lock was followed by the knob turning. Hyacinth stepped into the kitchen, and Polly fell, sobbing, into her arms.

A rush of energy pulsed through Hyacinth. Not time for sleep after all. Polly needed her.

Hyacinth gave her a short, tight hug then stepped back. "Are you hurt? What are you doing downstairs? Why was the door locked? What's happening?"

Polly began in a whisper, "He's here. In the house."

She did not need to ask who Polly meant. James.

Polly went on, a catch in her voice. "Aunt Ellen told me to—"

A loud and unfamiliar burst of sound cracked and echoed through the halls of the manor.

Polly's face fell, and she began to moan. Eyes wide, she looked to Hyacinth. "Was that a gunshot?" She wrapped her arms around herself, as if her movement could negate the sound they both heard.

Though Hyacinth was sure that it had indeed been a shot, she shook her head, grabbed Polly by the hand, and pulled her from the kitchen toward the entry hall. She didn't know what Polly thought Mrs. Carter wanted her to do, but Hyacinth was not about to leave her alone anywhere in the manor. If James was in the house, everyone was in danger, and she would not leave Polly by herself.

The girls ran for the front of the house, Polly moving as quickly as Hyacinth, as fast as Hyacinth had ever seen her glide over carpeted hallways and forested trails. They skidded to a sudden stop in the entryway between the beautiful staircases.

"Which one?" Polly asked, glancing between the north and south wings. Neither hallway gave a hint of lamplight. The halls were as dark as ever. How could they know which way to go, which hall to search? Was Lucas up one of the stairways? Was Mrs. Carter? Was James?

Hyacinth silently cursed the architect who had envisioned Ashthorne's glorious, sweeping entryway and its impractical staircases.

If the sound they heard only a moment ago had, in fact, been a gunshot, they did not have time to make the wrong choice.

"We must think. What does he want?" Hyacinth asked, but as soon as she said the words, they both knew the answer.

"You," Hyacinth said.

"Me," Polly answered.

Hands still joined, they ran up the forbidden north staircase.

At the top of the stairs, they ran a few steps, and both stopped short and stared at the floor in horror. Even in the darkness, there was no doubt. Hyacinth and Polly fell to their knees on either side of Lucas Harding's body.

All the breath left Hyacinth's lungs. She could not match the keening moan Polly made, for there was not enough air to make a sound. Her heart slammed against her ribs, painful from the inside.

How could this be?

She brought her hands to her face, her fingers covering her mouth as if to stop a scream from forming.

Polly dropped her head to her brother's chest and wailed, her arms reaching around his still form.

Hyacinth searched his face. That tumble of dark waves pushed back now as he lay with his face to the ceiling. His eyebrows, those perfect frames for the eyes that would never open again.

The lips that had spoken soft words into her ear, that she had so often kissed.

As her eyes scanned the beloved face, she felt her lungs compress even more. The loss of Lucas Harding changed the very air around her, making it heavy and thick. Filled with rage and grief, Hyacinth wondered if she would ever be able to breathe again.

Polly wailed and seemed to try to lift Lucas into her frail arms.

Eyes closed, Lucas flinched, and his brow wrinkled in pain.

Hyacinth gasped and placed her hand on Polly's back, but the woman shook her head and pressed her face into her brother's shoulder.

"Polly. Look," Hyacinth said.

Polly raised her head a few inches, and Hyacinth gestured to Lucas's grimace of pain.

Of course Hyacinth did not want to see him injured, but the rush of relief she felt knowing he was alive filled her with hope. She would not push Polly aside, but Hyacinth needed to touch Lucas, to feel his heart beating. To know she was not imagining his survival. She placed her hand at the cuff of his jacket.

"Lucas," Polly whispered.

He moaned in reply. Hyacinth felt a sigh escape her. Alive and responsive.

Polly sat up and clutched Lucas's hand. "Lucas, Lucas, my

dear, oh Lucas." Her relief and her fear were as plain to read as if they were inscribed on her skin.

With visible effort and after what seemed like a very long time, he opened his eyes. Panic flooded his expression as he took in the sight of the two women surrounding him. He struggled to sit up.

"Shh," Hyacinth said, moving her hand to his shoulder. "Where are you hurt?"

Propped on one elbow, he glanced down at his leg where a dark, wet spot spread across the middle of his thigh. A small hole had been torn in the fabric of his trousers.

Hyacinth was sure she was seeing a bullet wound for the first time. She pressed her fist to her mouth.

Polly smoothed back Lucas's hair, her whispered words an unending stream.

He attempted a calm voice. "You both need to leave. Right now. Get out of the house."

Polly shook her head and gave a hysterical laugh. "We cannot leave you."

It was true. There was no way the women could turn their backs on this man who lay bleeding on the floor at the top of the manor's stairs. This man they both loved.

Only now did Lucas seem to realize that, despite his wishes and his direct orders, Hyacinth and Polly had come up the stairs together. He looked from his sister to Hyacinth and back.

Hyacinth knew they needed to move quickly. She said, "We have to get you out of this hallway. Give me a moment, and I'll open a door."

Only the thought of removing Lucas to a safer spot could

have induced her to step away from his body as he lay shuddering on the ground.

Fingers trembling, Hyacinth plucked a pin from her hair and walked to the second door. The first room was the one she'd found ransacked, and she wanted to settle Lucas in a room with less obvious damage. Someplace peaceful. Someplace James had not destroyed.

Standing with her back to Polly and Lucas, she heard their whispers, the familiar speech between cherished siblings, and felt a tug at her heart. She loved the way Lucas so obviously adored his sister, and Polly couldn't cherish Lucas more. Their mutual devotion was admirable, and it made Hyacinth wish she had a stronger connection with her brother and sister.

She wiggled the pin in the lock, but her hands shook and the delicate wire missed the locking mechanism. She couldn't get the tumblers to turn. Pulling the pin out of the lock, she shook her arm as if ridding her sleeve of an insect and tried again. When her second attempt was no more successful than the first, she let out a frustrated sigh.

She felt a soft touch on her arm. Polly stood beside her, holding a ring of keys in her hand. Of course Polly had a set of keys. She had permission and ability to go anywhere she wished. The north wing of Ashthorne was not forbidden to her.

Hyacinth stepped out of the way, and Polly unlocked the door. "Thank you. Will you see if the room is in acceptable condition? If the bed is usable?"

Polly seemed to understand what Hyacinth was asking. Surely she had seen the mess James had left in the other room. And his warning note. He could get into locked rooms as well, Hyacinth realized. He had proved he could access any space in the manor. He might be in any room, in front of them or behind them. The thought made her ill.

Hyacinth moved back to Lucas, who was still attempting to sit up. She saw the strain in his face and imagined the tremendous pain he must be feeling.

Before she could ask him anything, he reached up and took hold of her arm. She felt his fingers trembling.

"Please take Polly away," Lucas said. He met her eyes with ferocious intensity. "Please. Do this for me. Get her someplace safe. She's in danger, and she won't leave me unless you take her."

"You're right. She won't." Hyacinth did not say that she did not have any plan to leave him either.

He spasmed in pain. His voice came out with puffs of breath, as if his lungs were powered by a steam engine. "She must speak out against the company she worked for. The world needs to know about the dangerous factory conditions."

He flinched at some unseen pain, and Hyacinth tried to press him back to the ground. He shook his head and continued, as if his words could help his sister's cause. "It's because of her work for those people that she suffers now. Chemicals she used to make matches poisoned her, and now she will die far too young and in a great deal of pain."

Hyacinth placed her hand on his forehead, hoping to transfer some of her strength to him.

He closed his eyes. His frustration was apparent, but Hyacinth was unsure if he was irritated by his inability to stand up and chase after James or because she was not eagerly agreeing with him.

He looked toward the room Polly had entered to prepare for him. Lowering his voice to keep the conversation between him and Hyacinth alone, he said, "She has to show her face. She must speak about what happens to the girls who do this work. She can show the world what the poison has done to her and what it did to Rosa. To who knows how many others. Her story can force the entire industry to change. That is power. She is dangerous to the company, and they want to silence her." He shifted his weight to one side and grimaced. "These threats and warnings were only the beginning. The man has a revolver, and he is willing to use it." Lucas gestured to his leg. "He shot me, and I'm not the one whose face carries the evidence."

He gripped her arm more tightly. "Please, Hyacinth. Take her away. Protect my sister. I can't lose her now—not this way."

"Nobody's losing anyone," Hyacinth said, her voice clipped. His words affected her in so many ways, she was unable to comprehend them all. She felt all the passion of his conviction. He was certain he was right about the threat to Polly's life, as well as about how she could inspire manufacturing safety reform in the match factories if she was allowed to tell her story. She heard his love for his sister, and she understood he was counting on Hyacinth to save Polly. Most of all, he feared what James might do when he crossed Polly's path again.

She could not promise to protect Polly, but she could promise to try.

"Can you stand?" she asked.

"I think so, but I'll need your help."

Lucas had kept secrets from Hyacinth, and he had de-ceived her. But understanding as she did now that he had done so in protection of his sister, Hyacinth felt all her resent-ment toward his actions disappear. He needed her, and she wanted nothing more than to help him.

With some maneuvering, she managed to get Lucas up and balanced on one leg, her arm around his waist. Looking over her shoulder, she asked, "Which way did he go?"

Lucas winced and turned his face from her. "I'm sorry. I didn't see."

Hyacinth drew in a deep breath. A menacing man with a weapon lurked somewhere in the vast expanse of the dark and silent manor. Any turn around a corner or opening of an unlocked door might bring them face to face with him. But the fact that he had not made an attempt to capture Polly here in the hallway at the top of the stairs suggested he was elsewhere, at least for the moment.

Hyacinth knew this might be their best, maybe their only, reprieve.

Together, leaning on one another, they hobbled into the unlocked room and found Polly turning down blankets on the bed. Cast-off dust covers lay in piles on the floor. Polly rushed to Lucas's other side, and together the three of them got Lucas settled in the bed.

Polly climbed up and sat beside him.

Lucas shook his head. "You can't stay here. I need you to go."

Polly shook her head just as emphatically as her brother

had. "I heard you when you said that earlier. And now it is my turn. You must hear me. I will not leave you."

Lucas's eyes looked wild. "Polly, please."

Hyacinth watched as determination settled on to Polly's disfigured face. "There is not an argument in the world that will convince me to walk out of this room." Polly placed the back of her hand on Lucas's forehead as if to feel for a fever.

He reached up and took Polly's hand in his. "He will hurt you."

Maybe it was the repetition. Maybe the sight of Lucas's leg soaked in blood. Maybe the tone of his voice, soft and filled with pain. Whatever it was, Hyacinth understood to her core what she had managed to ignore until now.

James was willing to kill any or all the inhabitants of Ashthorne Hall to keep Polly Harding silent.

LAMENT

I miss all that I once had.
So much that I fooled myself
Into thinking there was nothing left to lose.
Now I know that without him
Life will be unbearable.
Without him,
There is truly nothing for me.

CHAPTER 19

Hyacinth could not stand still and listen to Polly argue with her brother about his safety versus her own. She went to the pile of dust covers in the corner and pulled a sheet into her arms. With the help of her teeth, she tore a notch in one of the furniture covers and ripped a long strip.

Returning her attention to the Hardings, she noticed Polly looked more heartbroken than angry, tears in her eyes, and Hyacinth wondered if Lucas was succeeding in convincing his sister to leave the manor and save herself.

Without interrupting and not daring to intrude on the discussion, Hyacinth approached the side of the bed and began tucking the strip of cloth beneath Lucas's leg.

Standing as close as she was, Hyacinth could not pretend she wasn't listening to the argument when she heard her own name.

"Hyacinth will escort you off the estate," Lucas said.

Her instinct was to fight back, to say, "No, Hyacinth will do no such thing," but she began to realize Lucas was probably right—Polly was not safe in the house as long as James could enter, and Polly would be far safer if Hyacinth accompanied her than if she headed off toward the village on her own.

As if thinking of James conjured him out of the air, Hyacinth heard sounds of stumbling and cursing through the wall. Somehow James had entered the servants' hallway between the bedrooms and the outer walls. A powerful crash against the connecting door gave them all a shock, and Polly squeaked in surprise. Lucas shook his head at his sister, and she covered her mouth with her hands.

The door held, and James moved on.

Lucas's gaze seemed to follow the wake of the scuffling sounds, and as soon as the noises passed out of hearing, he whispered, "You have to go now. Take the hidden staircase and get as far away as you can. Go the opposite direction." He pointed south.

Taking the ends of the cloth Hyacinth had torn, Lucas tied a knot around the wound on his leg. His face drained of any remaining color, and he looked seconds from fainting. The compression of the tied rag might slow the bleeding, but his pain would keep him from walking.

"I'll find you," he said, gesturing his sister toward the cabinet door that matched the one in Hyacinth's bedroom. "Hurry. Be safe."

With a sob and a lingering glance, Polly nodded and turned to the connecting door. Finding the correct key was the work of only a moment, but Hyacinth took advantage of that moment to lean over Lucas and press a kiss onto his mouth.

"I'll come back for you," she said. "I'll take Polly some-place safe, and we'll find help, and you and I will have all the time we need to discuss the fact that you will never lie to me again—nor will you stand in the way of any more bullets. As it turns out, I'm not sure I can live without you."

Without waiting for him to reply, she kissed him one more time and ran into the servants' hallway with Polly. Hand in hand, they raced along the narrow passage to the first landing, where they took the turning that would lead them back to the kitchen and out into the night.

Hyacinth threw the door open and saw the kitchen floor littered with fragments of what appeared to be every breakable dish, plate, and teacup left in the Whitbeck's collection. Between the time Polly had let Hyacinth in the locked kitchen door and when James stumbled past the room where Lucas lay, the man had broken and scattered enough of the family's porcelain to cover every inch of floor with sharp shards.

Hyacinth shook her head. "Your slippers won't protect you against this, and I don't have the strength to carry you," she said. "We can't go out through this door."

Polly tugged at Hyacinth's sleeve and pulled her back into the servants' staircase. "Come with me," she said.

Back in the landing, facing three other doors, Polly pointed to the middle one. She leaned her ear against the wood, and Hyacinth followed. They listened intently, and no sounds of pursuit came.

"Do you know which one leads where?" Hyacinth asked.

Polly nodded. "This is the one we want."

"Do we need a candle? A lamp?" Hyacinth remembered opening the doors, the darkness. The chill and damp.

Polly reached over and took Hyacinth's hand. "All we really need is to hurry."

She couldn't argue with that logic, and Polly unlocked

the door. They ran through the door and down the stairs. The stairway narrowed as they descended, pressing the two of them closer together.

Hyacinth's nose filled with the damp scent of rain on stone, surely an effect of the humidity of the passageway. As the air grew colder she wondered where they were heading. Did the staircase lead to the cold storage area she had previously discovered but left unexplored?

Perhaps another complete level of the house, rooms left vacant and undisturbed, bearing only remnants of former generations. What might rest in such a space? And what might linger in a state of unrest? Even though she understood the reasons Polly had stayed hidden in the north wing, she could not forget the ghostly essence of the manor house. Polly and Rosa may not be haunting Ashthorne Hall, but that didn't mean nothing was.

Hyacinth and Polly moved faster as the stairs took them lower, and soon Hyacinth noticed she could no longer hear the whisper of the wind that always whistled and wailed through the halls of Ashthorne. She pulled against Polly's hand to stop her.

"Can you hear anything?" she asked, feeling relieved by the sound of her own voice.

Polly shook her head. "Is he following us?" she asked, trembling.

"No. It's so quiet." *Too quiet*, Hyacinth thought. *Too unfamiliar.*

Polly said, "We're underground."

Now that Hyacinth connected the quiet with being below the surface, the silence felt oppressive, suffocating, as if the breezes in the halls must still surround her, but something prevented her from hearing or feeling them. A shudder overtook her, and she reached out her hand again to trace the stones of the wall beside her, hoping to anchor herself. The stones wept with damp, and Hyacinth recoiled and wiped her fingers on her skirt.

No door and no wall appeared in front of them as they moved on, only more and more stairs. Hyacinth attempted to keep her imagination in check, forcing herself to keep one hand in Polly's and the other on the wall. How far could this staircase continue?

The darkness drew as close as the walls beside them, obscuring the stairs in front of their feet. Whenever Polly opened her mouth, her gums shone with an eerie green glimmer. Hyacinth had seen it before, but the shadows of the hallway made the glow appear bright. Had she not known what she witnessed, Hyacinth would have been frightened. She *had* been frightened, she reminded herself, when she'd first seen the unearthly greenish-white light in the dark halls of the manor house.

Lower and lower they descended, until once again, air moved past their skin as if the passageway itself were breathing.

Blood rushed in her ears, in and out with each step. Only when it grew louder did she realize that the sound she heard was not inside her head at all, but on the other side of the stone wall. The sea.

"Do you hear it?" Hyacinth asked.

"Waves," Polly said.

At last, the steps leveled, and Hyacinth and Polly were on a stone floor. As they moved forward, the walls fell away from their narrow confines, and at a curve, a patch of indistinct, subdued light appeared.

Polly must have seen the same thing, because she pointed with their joined hands.

"Is that the moon?" she asked.

Hyacinth gasped. She moved closer to the opening in the wall and squinted out at the night sky, barely brighter than the cavern in which they stood.

They had followed the staircase far enough underground that they'd arrived at the cliff wall.

Hands still clutched together, the two women stepped slowly and carefully around the perimeter of the grotto in which they found themselves. It was at least the size of Hyacinth's bedroom in the manor.

Hyacinth looked at Polly. "You knew about this?"

Polly shook her head. "Only that the stairs went down farther than I'd ever taken them."

"It appears we've found the end," Hyacinth said.

"What is this place?" Polly asked.

It was the most obvious question, but hearing it aloud sent Hyacinth's mind seeking data, interpretations, explanations, and answers.

Had the space been carved from the stone cliff? Had the rushing tidewaters eroded it away over centuries, carrying minuscule particles of stone and sand into the ocean, bit by tiny bit? Might a previous inhabitant of Ashthorne Hall have come down the long flight of stairs to fish at high tide? Did the family's servants toss their household waste into the bay? Did someone once use this cavern to stockpile treasure that washed up from shipwrecks in the cove?

She supposed any or all of those theories could be true, or perhaps none were right, and the explanation was something she had not even thought of. Perhaps Polly would give her another idea. The discussion would pass the time in any case.

She turned to ask Polly what she thought the space might be best used for, but instead of encountering the slightly glowing face she expected, the barrel of a revolver glinted before her eyes in the muted reflection of the moon.

Hyacinth's immediate reaction was to step in front of Polly and shield her from the man on the other side of the gun. Even the fresh air from the bay couldn't mask the scents of filthy clothing, tobacco, and stale whiskey. Without their notice and despite their precautions, James had followed them down the stairs and to the end of the passageway.

The very end.

He stood at the foot of the stairs, and there was nowhere for the women to go but out the cave entrance to the cliff face and the deadly waters far below.

Hyacinth had promised Lucas she would protect his sister, but there was so little she could do. She reached for Polly, taking her hand and attempting to shield her.

But Polly Harding was finished with hiding.

She squeezed Hyacinth's hand, and their eyes met. Polly held Hyacinth's gaze as if drinking in her friend's strength.

Then, Polly, head low and shoulders stooped, dropped Hyacinth's hand and rushed toward James, rising to her full height as she ran, extending her torso and raising her chin. She shouted, her voice crackling. "No. No."

Whether it was the speed with which she moved or his shock of seeing her glowing face, Polly's appearance startled James enough that he cried out, cursing, and dropped his revolver. The gun clattered on the stone floor of the cave.

James shoved Polly away and went to his knees to recapture his weapon.

Hyacinth stretched her foot out and kicked the gun backward, satisfied at hearing it hit the stone wall behind her.

James shouted, cursed again, and stepped forward, lunging for Polly.

Hyacinth backed up and lifted the gun, holding it in both hands. Her arms shook, fear and exhaustion draining her strength, but the gun remained steady, pointed at the man's heart.

In an instant, Polly ducked under James's arm and placed herself on the second step of the narrow passage, arms flung wide from her sides. Fierce light shone in her eyes. She gave a roaring shout that might have come from a mythical beast, so powerfully did it echo in the stone-walled chamber.

James stood staring at them, his head turning from one to the other. In that moment, Hyacinth and Polly had turned the tables, and the helpless girls he thought he had captured were now indignant warriors.

Hyacinth, knowing she must say something, opened her mouth to make her demands, but Polly Harding spoke first.

"I know why you are here," she said, her voice carrying the power of her battle cry. "You want me to be silent."

James stepped closer to Polly, but she did not cower.

Bracing her hands on both walls of the passageway, she kicked out one leg and caught him in the chest.

Reeling from the unexpected force of the frail woman's kick, he stumbled back, directly into the barrel of his own gun, held aloft in Hyacinth's hands.

Instinct sent him a step closer to Polly, but he refused to go nearer to her than that.

He shook his head. "Not me. I'm only the messenger," he said, a whine creeping into his voice. "It's the match factory owners who sent me."

He dared make excuses? Hyacinth wanted to spit on the ground.

Polly stamped her slippered foot onto the stone step. "Do not grovel," she said. "The company may have sent you here, but the company did not threaten me. The company did not trespass into my home, ransack our rooms, and shoot my brother." With each phrase, Polly seemed to grow taller, her voice growing stronger. Hyacinth had never heard such volume come from her ruined vocal cords.

"You cannot silence me. You don't want me to speak against the company? Now I will spread my story from coast to coast and around the globe. The world will know how you've ruined me. If you are truly only a messenger, then take this message back: My life is not over yet, and I plan to live until it is."

Hyacinth felt the hairs on her arms rise with every word Polly uttered.

"You gave me no choice. You would break into my house and threaten me until I yielded to your will. You used force. There was nothing for me but to be silent and run away or hide."

Polly leaned closer to James, her expression fierce and radiant. Each word came out as a shout, a call to arms, an anthem. "But I will be silent no longer."

Hyacinth's blood roared in her ears. She wanted to applaud, but Polly was not finished.

"Messenger, I am better than you and your kind. I will offer you what you did not offer me—a choice. You may exit this cave through the seaside wall, or we will put you in the ground."

Hyacinth gaped, her mouth hanging open in surprise at Polly's demand.

James shook his head, all bravado drained from him. "Just let me go." He pointed up the stairs behind Polly. "I delivered my message, and I'm ready to go."

She shook her head. "No, that is not one of your options. You will never sully the halls of Ashthorne again."

Hyacinth wanted to cheer.

"The details," Polly continued, her voice steady and firm, "are simple. When I say you may move, you will walk to the cave entrance and take in the scenery. Then you make your choice. We can shoot you here and wait a few hours for high tide, then roll your filthy body out into the water. The tide will predictably carry you away. It happens twice a day, every day. Dangerous waters here at high tide. Or you can take yourself out of this hole now and scrabble down the rock face while there is still a stretch of beach to make your escape."

Hyacinth stepped forward and placed the barrel of the gun against James's back. *Please*, she thought. *Please don't make me pull this trigger.*

With a nudge of the revolver, Hyacinth led James to the cave's opening.

James stood at the edge, head shaking in denial or fear. "There is no way to get down this wall," he said. "It's a sheer cliff."

Hyacinth spoke for the first time in many minutes. "There are several ways. If you brought a rope, you could lower yourself down. Did you bring a rope, James?"

He spat on the floor of the cave, but it was a weak attempt at intimidation. After all, she held the gun.

"There are also steps carved in the stone in several spots along the cove. Nobody wants to be caught on the beach when the tides come in, after all." Keeping the gun steady at his back, she leaned toward the edge. She felt Polly's hand against her back, and it gave her the strength to continue speaking.

"Go on, look. Just there, do you see? There's a step close enough for a large man like yourself to reach if you go out feet first. And enjoy the journey, because after your descent, you will not be taking steps along this cliff ever again. I will watch you until you round the corner at the edge of the crescent cliff."

Hyacinth caught Polly's eye, and they smiled at each other, an arc of strength reaching across the space between them. Polly's expression was radiant with her triumph, and Hyacinth thought her beautiful.

"You'll kill me either way," James said, the shake in his voice proving his fear.

"No," Polly said, her voice quieter. "We have honor. We keep our word."

"Go on," Hyacinth ordered. "Your time is running out."

James seemed to gather himself, then he sat on the ground and let his legs dangle far above the crescent of sand.

Hyacinth said, "Low tide will not last much longer. You need to move swiftly, but do not rush. The stones will be damp and slippery."

He turned over on his stomach and in a few seconds only his head and shoulders were still in the cave. Then only his fingers. Then, in an instant, he was gone.

Hyacinth's exhale was loud, but Polly's included a whimper that proved beyond any other indication how much her performance had taken out of her. Hyacinth set the gun down at her feet. She took Polly in her arms, gently enfolding her and whispering close to her ear.

"Polly, you were incredible. I have never seen anything like you. Please, sit down on the stairs for a minute." She walked with Polly and guided her to the makeshift seat.

She had no desire to pick up the gun again, but if James looked up from his climb and saw her without it, he might regain his courage and come back toward them. She lifted it by its handle and held it between her fingers like it was something filthy.

From the cave opening, she saw the man's figure in the night's patches of moonlight, creeping down the last of the stone steps far below. When he reached the beach, he paused and looked back up the cliff.

Hyacinth waggled the revolver so it would catch any moonbeam that might reflect in its metal surface.

James turned and began to run across the narrow crescent of sand, the tide advancing inch by inch toward the cliff walls.

Hyacinth watched him until he disappeared into the dark.

LAMENT

I may never again find the fire within myself to fuel such holy indignation.

Without the light of righteous fury, will I shine at all?

Will I ever again have need for a flame so vast?

Now I shall be content with a tiny spark.

A candle's worth to keep me warm.

Oh, but I am not finished with the flicker of my small taper.

Let me continue burning.

CHAPTER 20

Hyacinth walked across the cave floor feeling more exhausted than she ever remembered being. When she considered all she'd been through since the last time she'd slept, it was no wonder. This was surely one of the longest days she'd ever experienced, complete with more struggle and drama than she ever hoped to witness again, in her life or anyone else's.

Realizing the horrible man's gun was still in her hands, she stopped. Giving the spinning cylinder a push, she opened it and let the bullets drop into her palm. They made such a small clatter for such dangerous instruments. She put the bullets in her pocket and tucked the now-empty revolver into the waistband of her gardening skirt. She'd much prefer never to touch it again.

A sigh from the stairway entrance corner made her look up.

Polly sat on the stair, sagging against the wall as if she could not remain upright without the stones to hold her.

Hyacinth hurried over to Polly, searching the shadows to read the expression on her face. She was delighted to see that something of Polly's victory still remained.

Polly patted the step beside her, silently inviting Hyacinth to sit.

Shaking her head, Hyacinth attempted a laugh that came out more like a shudder. "If I sit down, I may never stand again. Can you walk up the stairs, or do you need a few more minutes' rest?"

Polly reached both her hands up toward Hyacinth. "Help me to stand, and we can walk together."

Hyacinth grasped Polly's fingers and guided her to her feet. Arms around each other's waists, they climbed the passageway steps.

She knew she supported Polly in their climb, but she also recognized that Polly bore her up. Not one strong and one weak. Both walking together, giving each other power.

Even so, the events of the night weighed on them both.

"Were there this many stairs on the way down?" Hyacinth asked.

"I believe so. At least, I don't imagine any have been added since we came down them tonight." Polly's answer was accompanied by a tired laugh. Her voice was raspy and crackling again. It seemed she had tucked away her fierce strength and power now that James no longer posed a threat.

"Is it still night?" Hyacinth asked.

Polly did not answer. The time of day or night didn't make any difference. No matter how shadowy the passageway, the darkness they'd been laboring under had passed. They put one foot in front of the other and rose toward the light.

Hyacinth wanted Polly to say something, to speak about Lucas. She wished she could comfort herself and Polly by stating her assurance that he was well, strong, alive. She was unsure, however, that her heart would survive the disappoint-ment if her hopes proved to be false.

So they continued to walk in silence.

At the kitchen landing, Hyacinth let Polly decide the path. The hidden hallway had been her purview far longer than Hyacinth had access to it. Polly did not choose to exit the servants' staircase or attempt to cross the kitchen floor still covered in shattered crockery. She and Hyacinth simply held on to each other and kept walking, all the way to the room in the north hallway where they'd left Lucas. Their exhaustion would wait. They both needed to know that Lucas was safe.

When they reached the door at last, Polly lifted the key, but only a bare touch was needed to push the connecting door open.

Stepping into the room, Hyacinth blinked against the light of what seemed like dozens of candles and lamps. Compared to the darkness of the passageway, the light blazed. Sounds entered her consciousness more slowly, voices talking over each other in whispers and in shouts.

The two women were immediately surrounded. A con-stable asked Hyacinth to follow him, but she simply handed him the gun from her waistband and dropped the bullets into his hand. She pointed to the staircase. "He's gone. Out a cave and down the cliff."

That seemed to satisfy him, for a moment, at least. He motioned for another constable, and the two disappeared into the cabinet and down the servants' stairway.

From across the room, the bedroom door opened, and she heard Mrs. Carter gasp. "Polly," she cried, running to her niece and throwing her arms around the frail shoulders that had so recently been strengthened as if by magic.

As Hyacinth watched the housekeeper enfold her niece, moving so carefully as if Polly might break, it was difficult to believe the transformation she had seen in the cliffside cave. But she wanted to remember. She wanted to tell Lucas every detail of the way his sister rose up like a goddess to protect herself. How she'd frightened away an armed man. How she'd pulsed with strength. How she'd *glowed*.

She looked to the bed, but it was surrounded by people, so she could not see for certain if Lucas still lay there. Hot liquid fear rose in her throat at the thought that he might not. That he might have been moved, and where. Or why.

Before she could push her way through the crowd, hands reached for her arms, and Mr. Gardner stopped in front of her, his face frantic.

It was so late into the night it was practically morning, but he still wore his brown leather apron and his red stocking cap. He let go one of her arms and pulled the cap from his head, holding it to his heart. His white hair sprang up and bobbed as he shook his head.

"Oh, Miss Bell. I am terribly sorry. Please, will you accept my apology? I am devastated that I employed that man. That I trusted him. That I gave him access to this house or any part of the estate." His eyes shone with intensity and possibly tears. "I would never intentionally put anyone in danger, especially not you, my dear." He clutched her arm so tightly she could feel her pulse beneath his hand. He needed her understanding.

She could give him that and more.

She covered his hand with hers and forced something

approaching a smile. "None of us can be immune to the workings of an unscrupulous man," she said. "I do not hold you responsible in any way for his actions."

"But I should have known," he began.

As much as Hyacinth enjoyed Mr. Gardner's company, she did not wish to spend time discussing deception and dishonesty. Not when Lucas's well-being was in question.

She glanced toward the bed again, but it was still blocked by backs and shoulders. "Mr. Gardner, may I come see you in the greenhouse and we can visit over a cup of tea? Right now, I need to look in on the rest of the household."

"Of course, of course." He loosened his grip on her arm, sliding his fingers to hers and giving her hand a gentle squeeze.

At her shoulder, she could hear Mrs. Carter murmuring to Polly, and felt confident they were both reasonably well, all things considered.

Hyacinth's eyes slid back to the bed, where at last enough people had shifted position so she could see Lucas. His still form and closed eyes gave her a pulse of concern, but as long as he lay in the room, she could hope his eyes were only closed in rest.

She stepped around Polly and her aunt, but as she approached the bed, a hand reached out and pulled her to a stop. She turned to see Mrs. Carter, eyes shining with tears, a beaming smile on her face.

"Dear, dear girl," Mrs. Carter said. "I cannot thank you enough for the way you managed to save Ashthorne tonight."

Hyacinth opened her mouth in surprise at the housekeeper's warmth, then closed it again against the denial she wanted to make. Save Ashthorne? She had done no such thing. Mr. Whitbeck's orchid collection lay in ruins. Lucas was shot. Polly remained standing only because of someone else's support. Rooms were in disarray. Heaven forbid anyone needed refreshment, because all the teacups lay in fragments on the kitchen floor.

And Hyacinth had been unable to stop any of it.

She knew she must answer Mrs. Carter's gracious comment, so she smiled and said, "I do love this house and the family within it."

Now the tears fell from Mrs. Carter's eyes. "For as long as you will have us, we are honored to be yours," she said.

A voice spoke from behind Hyacinth's back. "Aunt Ellen," Lucas said, "please don't frighten Hyacinth away before I have a chance to speak to her."

With a flutter of her hands and a giggle quite out of character, Mrs. Carter nodded. "Of course not, Lucas."

She clapped her hands twice to capture the attention of the people in the room, most of whom Hyacinth now saw only peripherally. She had eyes only for Lucas, who was surrounded by constables and at least one doctor.

"Mr. Harding requires a moment," Mrs. Carter said, her voice quiet and clipped, and Hyacinth thought she sounded much more like herself. With a backward glance and a smile for Lucas and Hyacinth, Mrs. Carter put a supportive arm around Polly and bustled everyone out of the room.

Hyacinth approached Lucas, his head and shoulders propped on cushions. His eyes had not left hers since she turned around, and now a smile began to grow. How had Hyacinth ever imagined a happiness that had not come directly from that smile?

"You look much better," she said, reaching out and moving a lock of his hair away from his eye. What gave her permission to touch him like this? Whatever the source, she relished her ability to do it.

His eyes sparkled. "Did I have you worried?" he asked through his smile, reaching up and pulling her hand into his own. He placed a whisper-soft kiss on her fingers.

Hyacinth might have teased in return had she not been so exhausted. "A bit."

He chuckled. "Only a bit? I got shot. I'd have hoped you'd have at least shed a tear for me."

Her answering laugh was no more than an audible exhale. "I've been a bit busy myself. Tears will come later."

Then, at the same time, they both said, "What happened?"

Lucas answered first, explaining how he encountered James while patrolling the upstairs hallways. He hadn't been sure James was in the house, but the wind made enough noise along those wide, vast corridors to mask the sounds of many intruders.

Mrs. Carter gave Polly instructions to stay near the locked kitchen door, and to open it to no one but Hyacinth. Then the brave woman put on a cloak and ran into the village for help. She summoned the constable, who telegraphed the coastguard station for assistance, and then climbed into his wagon with Mrs. Carter beside him. On the way back to the manor, Mrs. Carter demanded they stop for a doctor, just in case, and he squeezed in beside them on the bench seat.

"When she returned with her reinforcements, I was in this bed, barely conscious, and the house was silent. Even the wind stopped blowing. I don't mind telling you, we were both terrified. But of course, we behaved with commendable bravery."

Hyacinth laughed, knowing he hoped she would. In return, he pressed her hand against his heart. He gazed into her eyes as if it was unthinkable for him to look away.

Lucas seemed to remember that he was in the process of reporting his story. "By now I imagine the coast is crawling with searchers. I am so glad we did not need them to rescue you."

Hyacinth nodded. "I feel the same. But there is someone walking about out there I'd love them to find."

They shared a meaningful glance, and he gave her time to say more. She chose not to.

"But what about you and Polly?" he asked after a moment. "Stuck here in this bed, I thought I'd go mad with the need to run after you."

Hyacinth wanted to do justice to Polly's miraculous strength and speech, but she knew there would be time later to describe the scene in the cave. Years of time. For now, there had been enough fear. Enough excitement.

"I'll report the abridged version. We encountered James. He begged us to spare him, of course." She gave him a smile, half inviting him to take her comment as a jest.

Lucas nodded. "I believe you."

"We offered him options. He could exit the estate by way of the coastline and on foot, or he could stay and face the consequences."

Even telling the story playfully, the memory of what those consequences could have been gave Hyacinth a shudder of dread.

"And he walked away?" Lucas asked, shocked, as if there should have been more to the story.

Hyacinth nodded. Again, there would be plenty of time to explore every nuance of the story. Later, there would be additions from the constables who ran to the cliffs to find James. Later, there would be the perspective of time to add all manner of embellishments to the tale. Later, they would all breathe more easily. But right now, she hoped they could simply lay it to rest.

He seemed to understand her wish. With an exaggerated look of mock self-pity, he sighed. "At least he could walk," Lucas said. He gestured to his leg, immobile beneath the bed-covers.

Then his face grew serious. "This isn't the way I wanted any of this to happen. I'm so sorry. You know how the stories go. I was supposed to rescue you."

She was too far from him, standing at the side of his bed. Hyacinth let go of Lucas's hand and seated herself on the mattress beside him. For the sake of propriety, she kept to the very edge of the bed, but Lucas did not seem to worry they'd be interrupted. He moved over until they touched, but it was not close enough. With a bracing breath, he shifted again and reached for her. She placed her hand on his chest, and he took it in both of his own.

With her other hand, she ran her fingers through the waves of his hair, smoothing away the lines of worry from across his brow. "Perhaps," she whispered, her voice traveling no farther than his ear, "our story is different from others. Perhaps we rescue each other."

❧

LAMENT

With nothing left to fear, who am I?
My end will not change, but for my heart.
As my body weakens, my spirit grows stronger.
I am no longer alone.
I believe I am here to stay.

CHAPTER 21

Day by day, Lucas lay healing in the bedroom in Ashthorne's north wing, and Hyacinth and Polly sat by his side.

If Polly wished it, sometimes they spoke of her time in
the factory, standing at the dipping station or the match cut-
ter for hours and hours at a time, dreaming of what she and
Rosa would do on their day off.

Hyacinth held a book in her hands. Instead of field notes
and drawings of orchids, this one she filled, a page at a time,
with details from Rosa's and Polly's experiences in the factory—from the onset of their illnesses and their dismissal
from work to the damage they suffered from the match factory's chemicals to Rosa's rapid and painful end. Many times
as they spoke of this sad history, Polly shed tears, but her grief
was often colored by happy memories and the joy of speaking
of her beloved cousin.

Hyacinth added sketches and drawings, rounding out
Polly's stories with illustrations and diagrams. She was not
an artist in the traditional way, but years of observation and
note-taking helped her develop a talent for precision that

allowed her to document in words and pictures how Polly's physical impairments had progressed. Through careful revision, the notes became a detailed record of Polly's and Rosa's experiences. Together, Hyacinth and Polly prepared documents to send to solicitors and newspaper journalists.

They both recognized if the reports about this phosphorousborne disease and deterioration came only from sources loyal to the company, people like Polly and Rosa might be seen as tragic and pathetic. Even that their illnesses and death were sad but necessary byproducts of industry. But if Polly took charge and spoke up, she could use her voice and her experience to bring about changes. To protect other factory workers. To make a difference.

Polly was finished hiding. It was time. She was ready to tell her story.

During those times when Polly did not wish to speak of her past, the three of them made plans for the future. As often as she had time, Mrs. Carter joined them for an hour here or a few minutes there. She brought them breakfast and tea, and they all ate together.

Hyacinth still worked hours each day to repair the orchid collection. Incremental progress was slow in coming, but she knew the satisfaction of consistent effort.

A telegram to Mr. Whitbeck in India took her hours to compose and only seconds to send. The response was delivered to Ashthorne the next day.

Miss Bell,

A great tragedy about my orchids. They are my treasure. Please continue working on repair, replanting, and convalescence. Send a list of what was destroyed. I will seek out replacements here and abroad. Any orders you need to make, I approve.

Until we meet in the orchid house,

Whitbeck

Hyacinth handed the telegram to Lucas, who sat up in the bed. All the furniture in the room was now uncovered. Some of Lucas's favorite paintings hung on the walls, including a landscape of the property's little mountain. A cheery blaze glowed in the fireplace, and the once-locked bedroom now felt like a home.

"I'm glad to hear it," Lucas said. "I had no reason to think he'd be difficult about something that was not your fault in the slightest, but sometimes these great men become rather demanding."

Hyacinth stood from her chair and kissed Lucas on the cheek. "You're a great man yourself. Do you consider yourself demanding?"

He laughed. "I hope not. And you know very well I'm not any kind of great man."

She shook her head. "Untrue, sir. You are the greatest man I know."

He beckoned her to come close. She complied, but only, she told herself, because he could not yet leave the bed to move nearer to her. She looked forward to the time he'd again be able to make the approach himself.

Taking her face between his warm, gentle hands, Lucas

brought his mouth close to her ear. "I believe you are mistaken about greatness," he whispered.

She spoke seriously, but her smile colored her words. "Unfortunately for you, I have evidence and documents supporting my theory. You cannot defeat me in a matter of data."

"Granted. Is there any matter in which I *can* defeat you?" he asked, his own smile contradicting any hint of competition between them.

"Let me think," Hyacinth said, placing a finger to her chin. "At the moment, I can outrun you. I am much better at picking locks. I think we both agree that my songwriting skills are superior." She climbed up onto the bed and sat by his shoulder, snuggling in close. "But I concede that you have conquered me completely in every matter of love. You won my heart."

Lucas slid his arm around Hyacinth. "I hope you know how happy you make me."

"I've had a hint." She kissed him again.

"I have been lying here for far too long," Lucas said. "This bed is going to turn me into a lump. I really must break free."

Hyacinth laughed. "It isn't as though you are locked in here," she said. "If you're ready to get up, get up."

"Do you think I can walk?" he asked.

"I'm a botanist, not a doctor. I know nothing about the mending of bones, especially when they've been broken by bullets."

Hyacinth tried to laugh at the idea, but she had had nightmares of bullets and gunshots and holding a revolver between her shaking hands. She'd be delighted to never see a gun again in her life.

But for the moment, she could encourage Lucas to get out of bed. "You don't need to get straight back to mending the estate's fences. You could try moving to a chair."

He looked so hopeful at the suggestion.

Hyacinth slipped off the mattress and adjusted the pillows on the nearest seat.

Lucas held his breath and swung both legs to the edge of the bed. He reached an arm out, and Hyacinth stepped in beside him.

"Lean on me as hard as you need to," she said.

"I don't want to hurt you."

She nodded. "I know. We're in agreement on that point. But what's the worst that might happen?"

He gave her a rueful grin. "I lean too hard, and we both end up on the floor?"

"Yes. Well, let's try for a better outcome than that, all right?"

Days of lying still had made Lucas weak. Even sitting up at the edge of his bed seemed to tire him, but he drew in a deep breath and whispered, "Ready?"

Hyacinth nodded. "Let's stand up."

Side by side, wrapped in each other's arms, Hyacinth and Lucas stood together. He moved gently, favoring his injured leg, bending it at the knee and holding it a few inches off the ground. They both shook with effort as they hopped forward until Lucas stood directly in front of the chair.

Hyacinth said, "I'm just going to step out of the way, and you can sit."

Lucas placed one hand on the arm of the chair and

looked at the seat. "It's far away," he said. "I used to sit on chairs every day without thinking about it at all."

"You will again," she said.

He bent his good leg. It was more of a flop, and a bit of a crash, but Lucas made it into the chair.

Hyacinth clapped her hands. "Well done."

He shook his head. "It was no such thing."

"It soon will be," she reminded him. "Now where shall I sit? You seem to have taken my chair."

"I'd rather be standing," Lucas reminded her.

"And walking, and running, and riding a horse, and leaping over rivers. I remember. But in the meantime, I'd like to sit."

"I'd settle for a walk along the beach with you." He held his arms out, and she perched on his uninjured knee.

Hyacinth knew she would not always think of a dangerous man with a deadly threat whenever she contemplated the cliffs bordering the Ashthorne property. Today she would give her whole focus to the idea of this imagined walk with Lucas.

"I believe we could find you a cane somewhere in this huge manor house. As soon as the doctor allows it, we can begin with a few steps. Soon enough, we'll be taking the cliff-side stairs two at a time and running along beside the waves."

"Not soon enough for me," Lucas said.

"Granted. If we walked on the beach today, what would we see?" she asked.

He smiled and held her in the curve of his arm. "We would watch a cormorant hunt. He's clever at catching fish, but when his wings are wet, he cannot fly. So after his dinner, he stands on the beach with his huge, black wings stretched wide and waits for the sun and the wind to dry his feathers."

She hummed. "That sounds lovely. What else?"

"I would surprise you with a basket of sweet apples and a bouquet of gold and orange calendula."

"Fruit and flowers?" she asked. "How very kind. What's the occasion?"

"Our first walk on the beach in far too long," he said.

"Oh, yes. I agree. That is something to celebrate," she said.

"And if I could walk down the cliff steps, I could also kneel in the sand."

"Why would you want to do that?" she asked.

"This is an important celebration. One of us should be kneeling."

She stood up from his lap and knelt in front of him on the floor. He took both of her hands in his.

"And then?" she asked, looking up at the face she loved most in the world.

"And then I would tell you that I love you, Hyacinth Bell. That you have changed everything. You saved my life. You saved my sister. You make the world beautiful. You have shown me a new way to live and to love. And I don't want to be without you, not for a single day, ever again."

How was it possible her heart could hold so much happiness and not burst apart?

"How would you manage that, I wonder?" she asked, her eyes shining.

"That's the easy part," Lucas said. "By asking you to be my wife."

Hyacinth leaped from the floor and into the circle of Lucas's arms. "Do you mean it?"

"I hope you know I do," he said. "I adore you, Hyacinth Bell. Will you marry me?"

She drew her face close to his own, a hand on his cheek. With joy shining in her eyes and bubbling up from her heart in a laugh, she delivered her answer in a kiss.

EPILOGUE

Winter solstice. The shortest day of the year to celebrate the most wonderful event of her life. Hyacinth stood before the mirror in her room at the far end of Ashthorne's north hall and looked at herself in wonder. Her flowing lace gown peeked out from beneath a cape lined with the warmest wool. Even as fireplaces blazed and gaslights flickered with a golden glow, Ashthorne Hall still carried the chill of a wind that blew through cracks between stones.

A knock at the door signaled it was time.

"Coming," she called toward the door, turning to Polly Harding for final approval. She pulled back the cape to show off the lovely gathered waist, the lace at her throat, and the impressive bustle. It had been a long while since Hyacinth wore such finery, and she felt a bit sheepish at the extravagance.

"Will I do?" she asked her dear friend, the woman she worked beside in the orchid house and would soon call her sister.

"You are radiant," Polly said.

She reached around Hyacinth and lifted Eleanor. The orchid, housed in an outer pot of shining bronze and tied with a pink satin ribbon, boasted three blooms and two swollen buds.

Polly handed Eleanor to Hyacinth and smiled. "I know your mother must be so proud."

Hyacinth nodded. "Carrying her flower helps me feel like she's with me."

"She will always be with you." Hyacinth knew Polly meant what she said, and she also understood what was unsaid: that even when the time came that Polly's illness overtook her strength, she would never be far away from the ones who loved her.

Hyacinth leaned over and kissed Polly's forehead. "Ready," she said.

Adjusting the pink lace veil that covered her own nose and fluttered beneath her chin, Polly followed Hyacinth to the door. Rather than join the other guests, Polly had chosen to stay with Hyacinth in the makeshift bridal chamber; she would watch the ceremony from the back of the crowd. None of the guests would intentionally harm Polly or make her uncomfortable, but Polly chose her interactions carefully, keeping to small groups and quiet circles.

"I could not be more pleased that you are my sister," Polly whispered.

"I feel exactly the same," Hyacinth said. She opened the door to the hallway where her father stood waiting to escort her to Ashthorne Hall's grand ballroom.

Hand tucked into his elbow, she grinned up at her father, who looked as proud of her as he had always been. "Thank you for coming home from Provence to be with me today," she said.

"France will still be there when I want to go back. I wouldn't miss this day for the world. I am so delighted for you." He leaned over and kissed her cheek.

She could not hold in her happy laugh. "I appreciate that. I'm rather delighted myself."

He laughed with her as they walked down the long hall. "You have worked hard for everything you've earned. Your breakthroughs in botany are tremendous, and I couldn't be prouder. And the article you've written about the match girls will change the world."

Hyacinth knew his love for her colored his opinion, but she was aware that Polly's story could have lasting effects to the industry's workers and their rights.

Her father went on. "The things you achieve without seeming to work for them are even more precious. Your kindness, your heart, the way you love. And now, you're about to be a wife." He nodded to Eleanor. "I wish your mother was here to tell you everything you need to know."

She squeezed his arm. "Does anyone really know anything? I think the point of relationships is that we discover what works for us, one hypothesis, one experiment, and one piece of data at a time."

"You might be right," he said with a smile. "The next big adventure, eh, my girl?"

"There is much evidence to suggest it will be the best one yet," she whispered, her smile warming.

She couldn't imagine the smile growing any bigger, but then they crossed the threshold of the vast ballroom.

The enormous chandeliers held dozens of candles, raised to the soaring ceiling and glowing with warmth. Every uncovered window glinted in the midwinter light, weak sun reflecting off the icy panes.

Rustling gowns and the hum of muted conversation blended with the sound of violin and cello, and her father accompanied her past rows of chairs bedecked with sprays of holly leaves and hothouse flowers. Seated guests whispered as she passed, but she had eyes only for Lucas, standing in front of the vicar of Suttonsbury.

Lucas Harding, eyes shining and looking positively walloped by his good fortune, held out his hand as she approached. As their fingers touched, her joy escaped in a laugh.

Mrs. Carter, handkerchief held to her cheek, beamed at them through happy tears as she watched from the front row. The vicar spoke the wedding service, and Hyacinth tried to listen, but her imagination was full of the future.

Hyacinth looked down at her fingers, clasped in Lucas's. Together they spoke their promises. Together they took their first steps in the ballroom as a married couple. Together they faced a future filled with adventure and excitement they could not even begin to imagine.

$\mathcal{A}$CKNOWLEDGMENTS

It is such a great pleasure to write. I did not always feel this way, but I'm so grateful to feel it now. What a joy to have a job I love.

This book came about as a whim, a wish to share something amazing I'd read, a desire to try my hand at a new genre, and a nudge. Thank you to the ones who provided the nudges.

I have a terrific group of writer friends who read and laugh and suggest and commiserate and correct. For such a solitary job, writing has brought me so many dear friends and connections. Thank you to Brittany Larsen, Jennifer Moore, Jenny Proctor, Josi Kilpack, and Nancy Campbell Allen for braving early drafts and supplying unending support.

Thank you to the Proper Romance squad at Shadow Mountain books: Heidi Gordon, Lisa Mangum, Chris Schoebinger, Callie Hansen, Haley Haskins, Ashley Olson, Heather Ward, Breanna Anderl, Amy Parker, and Bri George. I love being part of this amazing team.

Here's a little historical note: Progress comes with costs. As the strike-anywhere match became a household necessity, factories on several continents produced cheap, accessible matches for the public. England's match factories employed mostly young women (small hands could manipulate tiny sticks easily) who were eager for work. Some of those factories abused their workers with horrible hours, inhumane conditions, ridiculous fines, and unforeseen medical dangers. After cutting and sorting matchsticks, the girls dipped them into a compound of sulfur and white phosphorus, which poisoned their bones and gums. Many people contracted phosphorus-based illness, and quite a few died. (When workers complained of toothaches, the company demanded they get the sore tooth extracted or lose their jobs.)

Diagnosis of this phosphorus-born illness came slowly. Doctors might not even have seen the workers until necrosis had ravaged the bones of their faces. Phossy jaw was a horrible disease, and iterations of it continued into later years. (If you're interested, *Radium Girls* by Kate Moore is a fascinating look at a following generation of women who painted glow-in-the-dark dials in watch factories.)

This story is set in 1887. Although we never name the company that employed Polly and Rosa, I've taken liberties with the amazing story of the Bryant and May match factory workers. In the summer of 1888, Sarah Chapman led a group of women and teenage girls to walk out of the Bryant and May factory in protest of their working conditions. This was a huge step forward for many industrial improvements as well as for women's rights. Their efforts were highlighted by social activists like Annie Besant, who ran the story about the strike in her weekly newspaper.

ACKNOWLEDGMENTS

There is still work to do. Progress continues—and still comes with great costs.

Thank you, family, for supporting me.

Thank you, reader, for coming along with me.

Discussion Questions

1. Do you believe in ghosts? Have you ever been in a building that felt haunted?

2. What do you think about the idea of love at first sight? Is it possible for a first impression to be accurate enough to build a relationship on it?

3. With a bit of evidence, Hyacinth allows herself to be swept into a fantasy of the haunted manor. How likely are you to dismiss scientific fact in favor of a feeling?

4. Setting is critical in a gothic novel. How did the landscape of Ashthorne Hall become a character in the novel?

5. Have you ever tried raising orchids? Did you have success? (The author has a black thumb and half a dozen bloom-less orchid stems in her kitchen. Feel free to reach out with any tips on bringing the flowers back to life.) What hobby are you passionate about pursuing?

6. Many of the events of this story are based in a character's fear. Were they right to be afraid? How did they overcome their fear? What are you afraid of?

7. Which characters in the story did you connect with most?

8. Several kinds of love are prevalent in the book: instant attraction, family pride, love for work, adoration of a sibling, romance, protection, and love of home. How do you see each of these leading to a successful conclusion?

9. Would you live in a nearly empty manor house? What would you absolutely require in order to stay?

ABOUT THE AUTHOR

Photo by Scott Wilhite

By night, REBECCA ANDERSON writes historical romances. By day, she sets aside her pseudonym and resumes her life as Becca Wilhite, who loves hiking, Broadway shows, rainstorms, food, books, and movies. She lives in the mountains and adores the ocean. She dreams of travel but loves staying home. Happiness is dabbling in lots of creative activities, afternoon naps, and cheese. All the cheese.

You can find her online at beccawilhite.com.